NOT YOUR ORDINARY WOLF GIRL

EMILY POHL-WEARY

SKYSCAPE

Text copyright © 2013 by Emily Pohl-Weary

Amazon Publishing
Attn: Amazon Children's Publishing
P.O. Box 400818
Las Vegas, NV 89140
www.amazon.com/amazonchildrenspublishing

Library of Congress Cataloging-in-Publication Date is available upon request.

ISBN-13: 9781477817308 (hardcover)
ISBN-10: 1477817301 (hardcover)
ISBN-13: 9781477816882 (paperback)
ISBN-10: 1477816887 (paperback)

Book design by Katrina Damkoehler and Susan Gerber
Editor: Robin Benjamin

Printed in The United States of America (R)
First edition
10 9 8 7 6 5 4 3 2 1

"IN WILDNESS
IS THE PRESERVATION
OF THE WORLD."
—HENRY DAVID THOREAU

CHAPTER 1

THE FINAL NOTES OF "Tenement Girls," my band's biggest hit, crashed into each other. Before the music could fade into nothingness, the crowd began to howl and smash up against the edge of the stage. I couldn't stop myself from recoiling. Screaming fans were nothing new, but they still made me want to duck and run.

My bandmates often accused me of being the worst rock star alive. Not the worst musician, fortunately. But I *had* been known to tell crazed autograph seekers to go learn how to play the guitar and leave me alone. I was a bit of a recluse. Okay, for an eighteen-year-old, I'd already developed some serious loner tendencies.

I also desperately needed to pee. My tongue felt like a boiled potato. White amoebas floated in front of my eyes, thanks to the glaring spotlights. One day I'd discover they were permanently burned into my retinas.

"New York, we love you, bitches!" shouted Jules Darling, our lead singer (guitar/keyboard), then she scissor-kicked in the air, oblivious to the fact she was wearing a microshort latex tutu. Or maybe *because* she was wearing it. Naturally, that made the crowd even more feral.

While I waited for the roar to subside, I focused on gulping mouthfuls of cool air and tried not to hunch into myself. Compared to Jules's outfit, my over-tight purple-and-red vintage Le Tigre T-shirt and black jeans were tame. I shuffled a few steps downstage, away from the white stone wall of the historic bandshell. Sweaty, writhing people stretched out in front of me, shouting for an encore.

I tried to be Zen-like, squinting at what lay beyond the bright lights. One of those perfect October midnights. The air was chilled and heavy. Dark mist transformed Central Park's grassy hills and fields into a slasher movie set. Shadowy autumn trees whispered that I could make it through this concert. Just ten minutes more and I could get off this stage. Thank god. My fingers hovered above Janis—my ruby-red bass guitar, named in homage of Lady Joplin. The audience held its breath. Jules signaled for me to begin the intro to our raucous encore, "Not Missing You." Her pointy-toed ankle boot tapped insistently.

I couldn't stop myself from peering into the front row for a familiar face. Harris Wall's brown hair was damp and flattened to his forehead, but that didn't make him any less delicious. He noticed me looking and finger-waved. Between sets, whenever the stage lights were dim enough that I could actually see more than ten feet, I hadn't been able to keep my eyes off the guy. Our manager, Vinnie, must've comped him. I made a mental note to ask that he be given worse seats in the future. It was hard to focus.

Sweat dripped down my forehead into my eyes. I squeezed my lids shut, focusing on the salty sting. When I opened them again and glanced sideways at Malika Stuart, our drummer, my face spasmed. After two years in the band, you'd think that I'd be done with stage fright. But I was still a total mess. Mali was a couple years older than me and Jules. She was a lot calmer about everything. She could make me laugh no matter what my headspace was like. She snapped one of her naughty school girl suspenders, winked, and blew me a saucy kiss, which forced me to crack a grin. At least my stupid face stopped twitching.

Some fashionista fangirls with asymmetrical hairdos pressed against the stage were close enough to witness our personal moment. They whooped. Probably thought we were in love. I grinned wider. Then the universe closed inward, sucked me into a black hole, and I forgot everything. My fingers darted across the strings and picked the correct notes. Then they did it again, and again, and again. Muscle memory was an incredible thing.

I was enthralled by the music and barely noticed Jules grinding and sashaying around the stage. I stepped farther away, out of the spotlight, to give her space. She deep-throated the mic and belted out the refrain: "You're not the one / I'm way off track / I need to get / My own life back / Go home, go out / Do what you do / Know that I'm / Not missing you!" The audience ate up the angry lyrics, as they always did.

And then it was over. Bam. I lowered my bass and mopped my wet forehead on the sleeve of my T-shirt.

"Good night, sleep tight, don't let the bogeyman bite!" crooned Jules over the mad clapping and whooping. That girl can make anything sound obscene. When the lights finally slammed off and the stage stayed dark, people were still going nuts.

I stood up from my half-assed curtsy and searched for Harris. He was talking to the people beside him: a younger blond girl with a boppy ponytail; a curly-haired, freckled brunette; and two guys who looked like brothers. They both had light-brown skin, dark hair, and chiseled features. The thinner one had been dancing by himself all night. The more muscular guy hadn't danced at all. In fact, he'd been perfectly still in the storm, staring up at the stage. Kinda creepy.

I'd been reading Harris's comic, *Dream Rage*, since it launched four years ago, and I'd been mildly obsessed with him since we met at a party thrown by my recording studio in the spring. Okay, more than mildly. If my crush were an espresso, it would be twelve shots strong. He was an incredibly talented artist. Not to mention a great dancer, in a spazzy kind of way. His perfect girlfriend, Marie, wasn't around tonight. She was usually superglued to his side.

Banishing thoughts of Harris, I unplugged Janis and hurried off the stage, pausing just long enough to use the bathroom, wash the sweat and mascara off my face, and put Janis safely into her case. With the bass hanging over my shoulder, I jogged down the hallway past the room where Malika and Jules got dressed. My nose twitched when a cloud of pot wafted out from under the door.

There was a maintenance exit up ahead that no one would expect me to come out. Between me and the door was one of the guys who'd been hanging with Harris—the muscular one with a staring problem—and the girl with a blond ponytail bouncing on top of her head. She spotted me and gaped. A fan. Up close, I could see she was wearing more makeup than Jules—it was literally shoveled on. When she noticed her guy was also watching me with an appraising look, she pouted, reached up, and tried to tug his face back toward her. His gaze didn't waver from my face.

He stepped forward and blocked my path. I hadn't realized how huge he was. Over six feet. Also gorgeous, in a hard, masculine kind of way. Not really my type. Refusing to be intimidated, I gave him a small shove and pushed past without slowing down.

"Sam!" he called out. "Wait! I came to this concert to meet you."

Make that *very* creepy. Shaking my head, I kept going and opened the door. A handful of diehard fans and a couple of photographers were waiting near the performers' entrance, hoping to ambush us. A burly security guard hovered there to keep them in line. Jules and Malika didn't have as many personal space issues as I did, so they'd go out that way.

As I considered my next move, the blond girl from the hall and her friend came outside through a different door. No sign of the guy. Snippets of their conversation drifted over.

"Jules Darling is the *coolest*," said the girl with the freckles. She was speaking much too loudly—deafened by the music. Maybe drunk, too. "Her hair, like, defied gravity."

"Ugh. Total hipster. All that blue eyeliner . . ." said Ponytail Girl, scowling.

"Her eyes were on fire! If sapphires burned!" the brunette said. "Those boots had to be real Chantays. I totally want them."

Ponytail Girl said something sarcastic, but too quiet for me to catch. Whatever it was, it didn't faze Freckles, who pulled a Jules-worthy scissor-kick. The bouncer frowned at them. Freckles smiled flirtatiously.

"Jules is a skank," said Ponytail Girl. "Everyone knows Sam's the talented one. She writes all The Puffs' songs."

"Yeah, well, I wonder who she was thinking about when she wrote that last one. I read on StarzStarzStarz it was Marco Belino."

"No way!" said Ponytail Girl, at precisely the same time I thought it. Freckles giggled.

Ha! As *if* I would write a song about him! He was sweet, and a decent singer, but 100 percent gay. When I was sure they were looking in another direction, I bolted. Phew! Having strangers gossip about my nonexistent love life was nothing new, but I wasn't going to listen to any more than necessary.

The tree coverage allowed me to skulk along the fence to my pink dragster bike, which I'd locked just up the hill. With Janis strapped to my back, I rode off into the darkness. So much less hassle to sneak away in the park than to escape from a packed concert hall. Most people took the closest route out to Fifth Avenue, because security ushered them that way. So I headed in the opposite direction and looped the long way around the park.

No sane person would choose to hang out here in the middle of the night. But then, I'd never been accused of sanity, and I didn't shy away from dangerous places. Biking around New York at night was my passion. In general, I stuck to the places and hours that other people avoided.

Once I'd put some distance between me and the crowd, everything became quiet. A dense chill pressed in on all sides, and I pictured a vampire lying in wait in the woodsy shadows. Silence was so rare in the city that it made me feel like the only living creature on Earth. My favorite view of the Big Apple was the one you got to see only in the wee hours. No traffic jams, business suits hustling the streets, dreamy-eyed sightseers, or fans hoping to snap candid cell shots.

The knots in my shoulders loosened. I was still getting used to my Clark Kent double life: bass player for The Cream Puffs by night and an intense introvert by, well, the rest of the night and day. We recorded our first indie album in my junior year at the Brooklyn High School for the Arts—Jules was in my year, and Malika had graduated the year before—got signed to a major label, and had been making artsy teens freak out ever since.

Yes, it was bizarre. No, I wouldn't give it up, go Howard Hughes, and start peeing in bottles so I didn't have to leave my apartment. I wanted the world to hear what I created, or else there was no point to any of it.

Vinnie whined that the audience paid good money to see our shows *and* watch Sam Lee, the Underage Troubled Rock Star, drink lemon mint bubble tea with her famous girl friends. When I didn't show my face at any of the after-parties, fans went home disappointed.

Truth is, I didn't really care what Vinnie said. I was never much of a badass. Schmoozing and being mobbed just messed with my head and interfered with making music. What I did care about was Jules and Malika's resentment about having to cover for me. But they were like family, so they usually forgave my oddities. Or gave me crap about them.

Other than my mom, who'd raised me, my bandmates were the closest thing to family I knew. My mother wasn't close with her parents, and my bio dad stuck around for only three years—the exact length of time it took to finish his PhD in sculpture at the New School—before heading back to Hong Kong. His number one passion was Chinese politics, and his sensationalist art had made him infamous back home. We kept in touch, but he'd only visited me a few times, when his work was part of an exhibit here. Not that I missed him. He was a stranger.

After being onstage, I was fired up inside and channeled that energy into my muscles. I decided to loop north through the park again so that I could enjoy the solitude a little longer. Streetlamps and light from the surrounding buildings illuminated the path ahead. I pushed the pedals faster and faster, ignoring the slight stiffness in my legs. Wind whipped my skin, made my T-shirt flap like a sail, and scrubbed away the smell of my sweat and other people's smoke and alcohol.

I rode or walked home whenever we played locally—it gave me a chance to go over the songs while they were fresh in my mind. I fine-tuned by obsessing over every sweet chord we hit and each fumble we made. We'd tried two new pieces tonight. One of them, "Dirty Street," still needed tweaking. My fingers itched to play through the kinks in the melody.

My thoughts bounced back to Harris. We'd recently hired him to animate parts of a video for a song called "The Spectacle," which meant we'd been working pretty closely together. I gave him concepts and went over his drawings. Collaboration only fed my massive crush. He genuinely cared about my inspirations and didn't seem threatened by The Puffs' success. As my amateur-philosopher mother loved to remind me: "An excess of good fortune is both a blessing and a curse." One of those curses was that most guys my age were either too threatened or too awed by my lifestyle to just be themselves.

I couldn't let myself think about Harris in a serious way, though, because he and Marie had apparently been together since kindergarten. An evil voice in my head piped up that she hadn't been at the concert tonight. But I was a girl's girl, which meant my loyalty had to be with Marie. I'd never put the moves on a guy who was taken. I'd have to be content with friendship and reading new installments of his comic.

Sighing, I leaned into a steep hill and veered off the path. Riding on the grass was totally against the rules but so much fun. My wheels bounced wildly on the uneven soil as I cut south across a field. The fog was thick. I could hardly see what lay ahead of me. Anticipating obstacles at top speed was like riding the ancient Cyclone roller coaster at Coney Island, which always felt as if it were about to unhinge and spin off into oblivion. I ducked under a particularly low-hanging branch and swerved around a bench.

Suddenly, a drop loomed in front of me. The ground cut straight down. It was too late to use my brakes. I was about to hurl off a mini-cliff covered with long grass and shrubs. My tires left solid ground. I jerked the handlebars upward, hoping to clear the foliage.

My back wheel snagged on a bush and stopped turning. The front tire slammed down and bounced to the right, and I got tossed face-first into the brush. Janis smashed into my spine. My hands tore through the grass as I desperately tried to grab anything that would stop me from sliding. A sharp something jabbed into my ribs. Searing pain shot through my chest. Then my head snapped forward and the world went black.

I opened my eyes. At first I didn't remember where I was. Then I shook my head, winced at the throbbing in my temples, and realized the source of my pain was a tree stump. My bike lay nearby, gleaming in the light of the full moon, taunting me. The park was still dark and silent. I rolled onto my side, groaned, patted my arms and legs, my face, then checked Janis's case. Nothing seemed broken. But my palms were scraped up pretty badly, and a goose egg had formed on my forehead.

I staggered to my feet. A wicked charley horse wobbled my left leg. Must have hit my thigh during the tumble. I checked my watch. I couldn't have been out for more than a few minutes.

Freeing the bike from the foliage with a vicious yank gave me small satisfaction. But it also hurt my scraped hands. Cursing at the top of my lungs, I limped down to the path and began to walk with my bike, hoping to work out some of the pain in my leg and thankful no one was around to witness my humiliation. Photos of me passed out in a bush would be Gawker material.

A few moments ago I'd been one with the universe. Now I wanted to throw my bike into a Dumpster and catch a cab home. I kept walking.

Something howled nearby, making the little hairs on the back of my neck jump to attention. Twigs crackled and snapped. Wet snarfling noises came from the shadows. I quickened my limp to an awkward jog. That was no lost Chihuahua. Maybe a rabid German shepherd?

A giant dog jumped out from between the trees, gnashing its big teeth. It had shaggy dark-brown fur. I wondered if it really was rabid. There didn't seem to be any foam around its mouth. I'd heard on *This American Life*—yes, I'm a closet podcast nerd—that infected animals were like zombies. They'll keep attacking until they're killed because their pain receptors have turned to mush.

Pointy ears flattened against its head, and its tail curled down between its legs. Definite warning signs of aggression. I squinted at the scruff of its neck but couldn't see any collar. The dog was huge. Maybe a husky. No, not a husky. Too big. Could it be half wolf? What color were wolves' eyes? This animal's eyes were brown.

My fight-or-flight instinct kicked in—late!—and I tried to detour around the thing. A terrifying rumble rose from its throat. It seemed to feel that *I* was the one who'd surprised *it*, not the other way around. Trying to recall anything else about animal behavior from my hours watching the Discovery Channel, I avoided looking at it directly, so I wouldn't threaten its dominance. When I headed to the left, with the bike between us, it moved forward, blocking my path. The throaty growl upgraded to a mean bark.

Screw the charley horse! I swung my good leg over the bike's middle bar; but before I could even get my foot onto the pedal, the animal bunched up its hind legs, sailed through the air, and slammed squarely into my chest. My guitar case hit the cement with a crack. I landed on top, with a bike wheel pinning my leg and the heavy beast on top of me.

Despite my panicked squirming, the animal calmly leaned forward and stuck its wet snout in my neck. Frantically, I rocked from side to side on top of Janis. Its maw burrowed deeper into my neck, sniffing loudly. I screamed and swatted at the animal's head with my free hand. My other one was caught beneath its front legs.

A second snarling dog emerged from the trees and leapt at us, smashing into the first dog and sending it sprawling. I could breathe again. The two animals rolled and skidded across the path, then jumped up, facing each other. Lips curled back, fur bristled, tails lifted.

I lost track of which dog was which. One of them growled. I expected it to lunge at the other one's throat . . . but it didn't. The tension abruptly ended when the one closest to the tree line turned and loped away. The remaining dog howled in that direction.

It turned back toward me. Hesitated an instant. I was too scared to move. Then, with a twitch of its tail, the animal sprang forward and sank its teeth into my forearm. I felt the pain before my brain registered what had happened. Its jaws ripped downward, tearing a bloody gash from my elbow to my wrist.

I began to shake and cry. I was going to die.

But then it raised its head, licked its bloody chin, and bounded into the woods. Sounds of crashing and running faded as the two animals moved farther away.

The world was silent again. I let out a slow breath and lay there for a few seconds, wondering if I was still going to die from blood loss. Far above me, two stars managed to shine through New York's perpetual layer of smog. That was enough. They gave me the strength to push off my bike and drag myself to my feet.

CHAPTER 2

A HOWL REACHED MY EARS from somewhere in the trees. It seemed like a good plan to get away before those creatures decided to return and finish me off. How many people came through this park every day? How could two violent animals like that be running around?

Maybe I'd hit my head harder than I thought?

My arm was doing a pretty good imitation of ground beef. I reached down with my uninjured hand and yanked the bike upright, gulping down my rising panic. If I didn't stop the bleeding immediately, I'd pass out alone in the middle of the park.

I leaned the bike on a bench, pulled off my torn shirt, and tied it tightly around the wound using my teeth. The pain was hell, but I could still open and close my fingers. A good sign. I just hoped it wouldn't affect my playing.

Using the bicycle like a crutch, I started down the path. After a few minutes, I felt strong enough to sit on the seat and weave to the Plaza Hotel exit, then made my way over to the bike path by the East River. It felt like the ride took forever. I couldn't stop seeing those teeth tearing through my flesh.

As I crossed the Williamsburg Bridge, the wind picked up over the river and buffeted me around. I was so disoriented, I didn't even think about calling someone for help until I was most of the way home. But the thought of facing curious fans was too much. And I didn't want to call my mom and try to explain everything at two in the morning. She'd freak out.

All I had on for a top was a black sports bra, which offered no protection whatsoever against the weather—or nosy fans. But by the time I made it to my neighborhood, I was sweating like crazy. The only good news was that my charley horse had disappeared. I couldn't grip the handlebars with my right arm, but I was able to rest my fingers there and work up a little speed.

When I turned onto my street and stopped in front of my building, I felt a lot less foggy. Heading inside, I noticed my T-shirt tourniquet was caked with dried blood. Grimacing, I wheeled my bike over to the elevator and listened to the outdated machinery thunder on its way down.

I probably should've gone to the hospital, but someone would recognize me, which meant questions and awkwardness. Besides, my arm didn't hurt that much anymore. When I got upstairs, I'd take a look and call my own doctor if I needed to.

My apartment was on the fourth floor of an old pickle factory converted into separate loft units. Six months ago, knowing what a mess the music industry's in, I'd used my share of the advance for The Puffs' next album, plus some help from my mom, to put a down payment on the building and soundproof my space. The other three floors were divided into two rental units each, which covered the mortgage. My mother lived only a few blocks away and helped me manage the property. It was a dream arrangement in New York, and the software business and clothing boutique on the main floor were no trouble. But if there was any way around the city's strict tenancy laws, I'd have turfed out the couple who lived beneath me long ago.

A week after moving in, the couple caught a photographer poking around their apartment, hoping it was mine—I'd dated another musician for about a minute, which made the paparazzi even more determined—and then my new tenants sued *me* for invasion of privacy. Like I invited the photographer inside! There was a reason I'd installed high-security locks. They were the ones who had the brilliant idea to prop open the front door of the building and leave their apartment unlocked while they took their annoying terrier to the dog run in the park. Luckily, the judge dismissed their suit with a stern lecture about wasting the court's time. Ever since, they'd been seeking revenge in petty ways: forgetting to date or sign their rent checks, piling their garbage *next to* the cans in the backyard, and running the hot water for hours.

The industrial elevator shuddered to a halt. Opening and shutting the rusty gate took effort with one hand, but I managed to get it so the thing could start its slow crawl upward. As I passed the third floor, I banged my bike's front wheel against the wall, knowing it would annoy the evil tenants, who slept close to the elevator shaft. I was nowhere near as schooled in vengeance as they were, but I had a few tricks up my sleeve.

The elevator finally stopped on the top floor. Ditching my traitorous bike with a kick to remind it that all was not forgiven, I made a beeline for the bathroom, setting Janis down on the way. My mouth felt like it was filled with sand—every swallow hurt—and I was worried I'd cracked my bass, but all of that would have to wait. I flicked on the overhead light and winced at the pain that stabbed my eyes. Were they more sensitive than usual? Was that a sign of . . . rabies? I searched through the medicine cabinet, grateful for my mother's neurotic streak. When I moved in, she'd stocked it to overflowing with first aid supplies. A few months ago, after reading about some superbug going around, she'd disinfected my entire apartment while I was on tour and added more supplies. My place smelled like hand sanitizer for *weeks*.

Before I could decide what concoction to put on the wound, I'd need to take a look. Gingerly, I started to tear off the fabric, which was plastered to my skin. Oh, god, maybe my pain receptors were already mush. I pinched my upper arm as a test. Ouch. Obviously, I had some receptors left. Maybe the bite wasn't as bad as it first seemed. Or my forearm was partially paralyzed. Could you paralyze part of your arm and still be able to use your hand to pick strings? Doubtful.

When I saw my arm, I was shocked. Instead of looking like raw, oozing meat, it was almost healed. I held it under lukewarm water for a minute and watched the flow turn dark red, then clear. There didn't seem to be any fresh bleeding, just a long scab that looked days old—definitely not an hour. Puckered skin on either side was red and tender to the touch, but the intense throbbing was gone. I felt better about my decision to come straight home, but what kind of wound closed up so quickly?

My palms were grimy. I scrubbed them gently with antibacterial soap, stopping partway through to gulp handfuls of water from the tap. My dry throat felt worse than my hands. The scrapes had already turned to spidery white lines. Even the goose egg on my forehead was gone. In its place was a purple bruise with yellowing edges. I slapped on a couple of different ointments that promised miracles and wrapped the arm loosely in gauze. I also slathered my hands with antibiotic cream to be safe.

In the kitchen, I grabbed a carton of orange juice from the fridge with greasy hands. One glass wasn't enough. I upended the container and stood there guzzling until I'd drained the entire thing. My throat stopped hollering for attention, and my stomach took center stage. A hunk of veggie pâté, some watercress, feta, and a cucumber went into a Jughead-sized sandwich. Afterward, I was still a bit peckish. So I made a second sandwich and devoured that, too.

I dumped my dishes in the sink, got a glass of water in case the thirst roared to life again, and climbed up to my loft bed. Exhausted, I drooped on the edge of the ladder and let my dirt-encrusted jeans fall to the floor. Even naked, I felt strangely warm. When I pressed my fingers to my forehead, they came away damp with sweat. Should I take my temperature? Call the doctor? Instead, I made the stupid and careless decision to give in to the siren song of sleep.

The instant my eyes closed, I was dreaming about misty trees rising from the darkness, abnormally large dogs with eerie brown eyes, and drunken hipsters gyrating to cheery estropop. At some point in the night, the images turned downright nightmarish: hairy, four-legged monsters chased me through desolate streets, jumped onstage while I was playing, and mauled my band—but left me untouched.

A sharp pounding woke me. My first thought was that my heart was beating loud enough to hear. I bolted upright, ready for anything, and saw that I was safe in bed. The downstairs neighbors were hammering at five thirty in the morning, settling the score for my elevator thumping.

The skylight above my bed filled with predawn colors ranging from dark blue to neon orange. Sunrise through the pollution. The banging stopped. I closed my eyes and tried to sleep a little more, but my nasty subconscious treated me to another disturbing slide-show. And I was soaked with sweat. Gross.

Peeking at my arm, I discovered it was completely healed. The only sign of the dog attack was a jagged, pinkish scar. My forehead wasn't even tender. That couldn't be normal. I climbed down from my bed and changed into yoga shorts and a tank top. While I downed three glasses of water and five toaster waffles loaded with raspberry yogurt and fruit, I worried about how far those downstairs neighbors might go for revenge. I lived in fear of leaked paparazzi photos. Once I'd had a photographer snap me changing in a dressing room after a show. There was only one way to see inside my apartment: through the windows four stories in the air. The couple could get onto the fire escape from their place. The clothes nook underneath my bed was fairly discreet, but the loft was open concept. Maybe I needed to invest in blinds.

I went into my office cranny and opened my laptop. I'd read in the *Times* about animal rights activists who wanted to reintroduce wolves into the Adirondacks in upstate New York. Was it possible that a couple of the creatures had somehow made their way south? The Internet didn't illuminate, though I found out the activists had given quite a nest egg to the cause—several hundred thousand. I tried to see if they'd followed through on their plan, but couldn't find any concrete reports. Anyway, those wolves would have to travel pretty far to get to Manhattan.

I was still feverish, so I gave in and took my temp. 101. A cool bath would help bring that down, but it wouldn't do anything for the temperature's cause. I popped three ibuprofen, submerged myself in icy water, and lay there until the shivering became intolerable.

Based on the state of my arm, no doctor would believe I'd been attacked last night. They were more likely to assume I'd slashed my wrist a week ago, and Twitter and the blogosphere would have a field day. Did I have to wear long sleeves for the rest of my life?

Vinnie was always pushing me to cultivate more of an edge. No thanks. I'd never get another second alone from the press or my mom. Not to mention I'd step on Jules's toes. She owned the bad-girl persona. Malika was the sexy, bookish one. And I was the loner tomboy.

I carried my bass and a two-liter bottle of soda over to the couch, where I flopped down and chugged until grape fizziness exploded from my nostrils. Setting aside the bottle, I opened the silver latches on Janis's protective shell, held her up to the light, and ran my fingers over every inch of her red surface. Not so much as a hairline crack on the instrument, though the case wasn't in great shape.

When it came to my bass, I was totally anal: it needed to have perfect pitch, look hot, and possess the elusive vibe that allowed me to picture one of my musical idols.

The effects of my cold bath were already wearing off, so I put away the bass and switched on the overhead fan. I didn't exactly feel sick, but at seven in the morning, alone in my apartment, the whole rabies theory was starting to feel like a real possibility. I went back to my computer. All the websites said to get immediate treatment.

The Puffs were beginning a video shoot, and I had to be at the studio by ten. I wouldn't actually have to play—we'd already laid down the track—but I would have to *look* like I was playing for hours on end. The gallons of sweat might become a problem. It was too early to call my doctor. The closest hospital was only a few blocks away. Might as well get someone to check me out now. Early morning on a Friday, the ER would probably be quiet.

I rolled my bike into the elevator and headed down to the street. As soon as I was riding, my body felt a million times better and I cooled off. I felt strong enough to keep pedaling all the way out to Long Island and back, but a nagging doubt made me pull into the hospital's driveway.

The admitting nurse glanced at my arm, asked for my insurance card, and listened to me babble about a dog attack. The look on her face said she didn't know who I was (thank you!) and she'd decided this was an elaborate scam to get a prescription. She told me to go sit on a couch in the waiting area. I sat there reading old *National Geographics* as patient after patient—who arrived after me—was led into the inner sanctum.

When I ran out of magazines, I stared dully at the lobby TV, wishing I had something to eat. They didn't even have a soda machine. A news report came on about some brutal attacks by a girl gang on the Lower East Side. A flash of fuzzy security camera footage made me curious to see the girls involved. I jumped on the couch to turn up the volume, and immediately wished I hadn't. Why was it so much more upsetting to find out females were capable of things like that?

As I was trying to make out the girls' faces, which were too grainy to see clearly, the inevitable happened. A teenage boy who'd broken his wrist in a skateboarding accident recognized me. I felt sorry for him and let his mother take a photo of us together with his phone. But when his mom stepped away, he started grilling me with questions like: "Is Malika Stuart gay?" and "Are you?" and "You babes are sleeping together, huh? That's so hawt." I wished I could delete his photo. If I tried to answer, it would just get worse.

Finally, the admitting nurse poked her head out from behind the automatic doors and called for me. I disentangled myself from the boy and sprinted across the lobby. A tired-looking doctor in her forties watched me approach through thick lenses, probably trying to figure out what the boy found so interesting.

I was sweating again at full force. While the doctor peered at my chart, I had the urge to snatch the smudged, crooked glasses off her face and snap them in half.

Whoa. Where did that come from?

"You're Samantha Lee?" she asked, glancing at the folder in her hand.

"Call me Sam."

"The musician?"

"Yeah," I said tightly.

She glanced at my fading forehead bruise and blinked. "I'm Dr. Alam. Follow me, Ms. Lee. We'll get you checked out."

She hurried down an off-white hallway with a green linoleum floor. While she walked, she glanced more closely at the papers in my slim file, reading the nurse's comments about my *fake* dog attack.

The stink of harsh cleaning chemicals assailed my nose. The smell of chlorine bleach was so powerful it felt as if my nostril hairs were being burned off one by one with a tiny blowtorch. I focused on holding my breath for as long as possible.

"Please have a seat," said the doctor, pushing aside the green-and-pink curtains of a makeshift exam room and gesturing at a bed covered in starched white sheets. I hopped up, earning a frown from the doctor. For a feverish girl, I appeared to be in pretty good shape. I slowed my movements and groaned as pathetically as possible.

"How're you feeling today?" she asked, tucking a strand of long black hair behind her ear.

While I'd been waiting in the lobby, I'd racked my brain for an explanation for my hospital visit that wouldn't make me sound like a lunatic. Judging by the nurse's reaction, the truth hadn't been very convincing, but I couldn't come up with anything better. "I'm feeling pretty weird. I've got this fever and—"

"The flu's going around."

I always hated when people finished my sentences. This time it made me want to break her neck. I took a slow, calming breath and tried again. "I was bitten by a dog last night, in Central Park."

"It says here you're worried you might have contracted rabies?"

"Right."

"Can I see the . . . wound?"

I shrugged off my thin jacket and held up my arm.

She peered down at the scar, then up at my face. "This is weeks' old, young lady."

"I swear, it's not. I was attacked last night by an enormous dog or wolf while I was riding my bike near the duck pond in Central Park."

She jotted something in my file. "You actually saw this dog?"

"Of course I saw it. The thing jumped on top of me!"

"Right, right. Why do you think it was rabid?"

"Well, it wasn't foaming at the mouth. At least not that I could tell . . . It was dark."

Her face twitched, as if she was repressing some reaction with great difficulty. "Did it exhibit unusual behavior, strange barking, lack of fear?"

"All of the above!" I said. "There's more. I'm weirdly energetic. Jumpy. So hungry and thirsty. Almost every moment, I want to shove something into my mouth."

Her eyes opened wider, magnified by her thick glasses. "Okay. Why don't we start by taking your temperature?"

I nodded eagerly. She removed an electronic thermometer from the pocket of her medical coat and stuck it in my ear. When it beeped, she inspected the results.

"You're a little warm," she admitted. "Nothing to worry about. Plenty of bed rest should do the trick."

"I don't have the flu! Aren't you concerned that a feral dog attacked me and chewed on my arm like it was rawhide?"

"Your wound is miraculously healed," she noted, raising an eyebrow.

"I swear on my life the bite was deep. I know it sounds crazy."

"Yes, it does."

"It's not completely healed." I jabbed at the scar with a fingertip. "Ouch! See, that hurts. Dr. Alam, is there any disease that makes you heal fast?"

"Why don't you ask Superman?" she said, then had the decency to look embarrassed. "Look, I need you to level with me. Is it drugs? Crystal meth? How about coke?"

"No! I'm telling you the truth. I was bitten by a—"

"Giant dog. Except that from the location of the wound, you would have severed an artery, which means you would have passed out within minutes. This injury happened weeks ago. Who did this to you? Are you covering for someone?"

"Not someone—some*thing*. There was a lot of bleeding. But I used my T-shirt as a tourniquet. Test me for rabies. Seriously. Please!"

Her eyes narrowed. In that moment, I truly hated her.

"Ecstasy? Or another street drug?" she asked.

"You think I *hallucinated* the attack?"

She sighed. "You seem fine, but I'll call in a colleague for a second opinion. Maybe we'll run some blood tests."

"Good, blood tests! You can check for rabies that way, right?"

She turned and left the room, shaking her head. I didn't care what she thought of my mental state—as long as she ran the actual rabies test. I spread my jacket on top of the hospital pillow, stretched out on the bed, and tried to play Tetris on my phone to keep myself from stalking around the ER.

CHAPTER 3

AFTER GIVING UP ON TETRIS, reading all the recent Google news alerts on The Puffs, and mapping the star-patterned pinprick holes in the ceiling panels for ten minutes, I heard footsteps approach my room. Two doctors spoke quietly, thinking I couldn't hear them. I could.

"I'm pretty sure she's on something," said Dr. Alam. "Her eyes are unfocused and red."

Excuse me?

"Drug-induced delusion," agreed a male doctor. "So do a chem test and call psych."

"That's the plan."

There was a grunt of approval. "And you're positive it's *that* Sam Lee? The girl my daughter's crazy about?"

"Not too many half Asian rock stars come through these doors. See for yourself."

I strained but missed the guy's response. No way was I going to let them take a drop of my blood! They were two seconds from shipping me off to rehab. I snatched my jacket, rolled off the bed, and landed on the floor with a muffled thud. Scooting backward, I folded my five-foot frame into a tight ball between the bed and a cabinet on wheels. Worst hiding spot. Ever.

One of the curtains swung open. If the doctors found me here, it would confirm their suspicions that I was a drug-crazed musician. But with any luck, they'd take the empty bed at face value and assume I'd split. I couldn't wait to get off this floor. I shuddered to think about the disgusting substances clinging to its tiled surface.

"Where'd she go?" demanded Dr. Alam. "She was right here!"

"Anyone see a girl leave this room?" hollered the other doctor.

Another voice shouted back—the ER nurse? "Sorry, I didn't see anything."

"Such a troubled young woman," said Dr. Alam. She sounded genuinely concerned. I almost felt bad.

"Telling my daughter I tested Sam Lee for drugs would've made *me* a rock star," the guy replied.

Patient files are supposed to be confidential! It took all my willpower to fume silently. I cursed the fact that I didn't carry a digital recorder. Once they'd walked away, I got to my feet.

Getting out of the hospital was *a lot* easier than getting in. Security didn't give a crap who left, and the admitting nurse was preoccupied with an elderly man in a neck brace bolted directly into his skull. Ouch!

Back on my bike, weaving in and out of rush hour traffic, I vented by swearing at cars. What a massive waste of time! Now I hardly had a moment to eat before heading to the video shoot in DUMBO. And I was starved again.

In my building, the elevator refused to come down and get me. Of course, the evil tenants had deliberately left the door open on their floor so no one else could use it. Locking my bike in the lobby, I hurtled up the four flights. In less than two minutes I'd inhaled a serving of day-old take-out noodles with spicy tofu.

I traded my sweats for skinny jeans and my favorite yellow T-shirt featuring a leprechaun dancing beneath the end of a rainbow. I shrugged on a jean jacket, slung Janis over my shoulder, and hurried back down to hail a cab and zip over to the production studio. The director expected us to be ready and on set when she arrived at eleven, and her team needed a full hour to get me dressed and done up.

When I tore into the studio, makeup and wardrobe almost lost it. I was sweating like a fountain, and my hair took "windswept" to a new level. But the team worked their wonders, tidied my short hair, powdered my shiny face, lined my hazel eyes with forest green, and painted my lips dark red. Luckily, the bruise on my forehead was now all but invisible, and they were too discreet to ask about my other scars.

A few minutes before eleven, I was alone onstage, dressed in a black leather mini that had probably been brought into the world as a belt, two dozen plastic bracelets positioned strategically on my right arm. I picked at Janis, trying to figure out how I could possibly still be hungry.

Then Harris wandered in. He crossed the room and stopped close enough for me to catch his scent, which was marked by a faintly spicy deodorant. I wanted to grab him and bury my nose in his hair. If he caught my eye, I wouldn't be able to hide the way I felt. I glanced down and pretended to be fascinated by tuning keys.

"Where is everybody?" he asked.

I reminded myself he couldn't actually read my mind. "Malika's in the dressing room. Jules got here late. She'll be in makeup for a hundred years."

"Ahh." He sat down cross-legged on the floor and took a sketch pad and an ink brush pen out of his canvas messenger bag. His curly hair flopped into his eyes as soon as he started to draw. He shoved it aside.

I shuffled a few steps to my left, trying to get away from his smell. And tripped over a cord attached to Jules's keyboard. Nearly went flying. Harris glanced up, then grinned at my dorkiness. *Slick, Sam. You're a real rock star.*

I prayed for one of my bandmates to come save me. Before I'd noticed how hot he was, being alone in a room with Harris was easy. Now that I wished his adorable girlfriend would fall off the face of the Earth, it made me break out in hives.

I fixed my eyes on the dressing room door and sent hurry vibes in Malika's direction. Jules wouldn't come out until the last second. She loved to make an entrance. And if the poor woman applied her makeup "wrong," which always happened at least once, Jules would make her start all over.

"Hope you don't mind me coming," said Harris, doodling away. "Vinnie said it would be okay. Seeing the shoot will inspire me."

"No problem," I said, craning to see what he was drawing. Was it me?

His head bobbed up and down as he scribbled, looked up, and scribbled some more. He *was* drawing me. I blushed, and my temperature rose another couple degrees.

"Did you leave early or something?" he asked. "Last night, I mean. You didn't come to the Cake Shop."

The Cake Shop is this bar on the Lower East Side that also has shows in the basement, and serves addictive cupcakes. Malika and Jules hang out there all the time. I have a love/hate relationship with the place because it's always swarming with people who want a piece of me.

"Needed alone time."

"You need that a lot, don't you?" He said it in a nice way.

"Guess so." A zing shot through my chest. He'd been paying attention! Then Marie's face popped into my head, and the zing turned into a pang of guilt.

Vinnie arrived in his usual used-car-salesman suit, along with our director, Spyke—one name only—who traveled with a pack of camera, lighting, and sound technicians. The crew all had choppy artistic haircuts, Williamsburg hipster outfits, and titanic lattes from a fancy Italian café around the corner. I used to find Spyke's warp speed refreshing. Today the gang's chattering grated.

Malika emerged in her New Wave school girl outfit: plaid mini-skirt that barely covered her butt; blindingly white, collared shirt that looked great against her dark skin; and fitted black sweater vest with an Anarchist circle-A stitched onto it instead of a school crest. Horn-rimmed glasses framed her eyes, and her full lips shone with gloss. She took her place next to the drum kit.

At last Jules sauntered out, wearing cake-like violet crinolines under a purple slip cinched at the waist with a wide gold belt. On her feet were dark-purple cowboy boots. Perched on her teased nest of white-blond hair was a sparkly lavender ten-gallon hat that would've been at home on a rodeo-themed stripper but also worked nicely with her eye shadow. Somehow she pulled off the look.

The stage lights turned on. I shifted into position, avoiding the electrical cord of death, and tuned out Spyke, who was barking orders at people. Someone played our recording of "The Spectacle." Any song will annoy me after I've listened to it over and over, and the goofy dance moves we had to do for this video didn't help. Screw catchy, juvenile tunes—my next song was going to be death metal. Ha! Vinnie would flip.

Since Spyke's over-the-top theatrical instincts were perfect for the song, I was willing to put up with her demands for take after take. But as the day progressed, it got harder to pretend I was having fun. The lights blazed above my head. I was sweating. Buckets. We got our money's worth from that makeup artist. By noon she had to touch me up after every take. I had so much makeup on my face, I'd have to scrape it off with sandpaper.

I finally lost it—on the four-hundredth run-through of a silly choreographed sequence to match lyrics about New York being like a circus. Malika pretended to walk a tightrope while I clowned around. Jules refused to play along, because all she cared about was looking sexy. She kept pirouetting with a hula hoop around her waist, causing Spyke to stop everything and make us start all over again.

"Oh, god. Kill me now," I snapped.

"What's your trauma?" Jules said.

"You're not six years old. That hoop is a terrible idea."

"Shut up. I *refuse* to look like an idiot in this video, even if you're okay with it."

"You're making the shoot take forever," I growled. Yes, growled— it began in my throat and ended as a low rumble in my chest. My lips curled back over bared teeth. Jules gasped. I smelled the sharpness of fear on her.

Vinnie recognized the warning signs of a band brawl and quickly announced a break. I leapt off the stage before Spyke could argue and dashed to the catering buffet before anyone else could get in line. Red-pepper-and-brie sandwiches, ordered specially for me, weren't going to make a dent in this ferocious hunger. I loaded a plate with roast beef wraps and chips, which made people's jaws drop—I'd been a vegetarian since I was twelve and watched a gruesome documentary on what life was like for cows at a slaughter-house. But today I craved meat. I tossed a heap of carrots on top, then added a turkey-and-Havarti sandwich for dessert.

Clutching two cans of organic soda in one hand, I sat on the floor in a dark corner, far from the stage, hoping it would discourage anyone from coming over to ask about my change in diet. I shut my eyes and relished the fact that the lights were no longer pounding down on me. Sweet relief.

When I opened my eyes again, Harris was hovering above me, holding a full plate. He hesitated, then sat down very close. If he moved just a couple inches to the left, his foot would touch mine.

"Must be hot under those lights," he said, picking up a pepper sandwich from his plate.

"The worst," I said from around a mouthful of beef, wishing he was a little less observant.

"So, did you notice my buddy's brother at the concert? I think he has a crush on you."

I wasn't sure how to respond. Was Harris trying to set me up?

"The guy who stood there staring?" I asked.

He nodded. "Owen Lebrun."

"Kinda creeped me out."

"He's all right. At least his brother, Marlon, is. Met the guy in a class about how artists have depicted the natural world throughout the ages. He's some kind of genius, doing advanced research even though he's only like two years older than me." Harris was slowly working on his undergrad at NYU, and his comic featured anthropo-morphized animals who talked to people—I could see why he'd be into a class like that. For a second I considered telling him about the attack; but if I showed him the scar, he'd think I was deluded, too. I watched him take a bite of his sandwich. I was used to being a loner, but I'd never felt this alone.

He peered sideways. "Hey, are you pissed at me for some reason?"

"What? No! Why would you think that?"

"You just seem kind of annoyed. . . . Hope I didn't do anything stupid."

I sighed. "It's not you, Harris. I just feel like crap today."

"You're kind of flushed."

"Fever."

He frowned. The expression just made him more adorable. "And you're still working? That's impressive. Also, I, uh, thought you were vegetarian. . . ."

"I was."

"Not anymore?"

"My body needs protein. Anyway, shouldn't you be worrying about your girlfriend instead of me?" As soon as the words popped out, I wished I could suck them back in. His frown deepened. Long brown eyelashes drooped to hide his eyes. "Sorry, that wasn't fair," I said. "I'm just a cranky jerk. I don't know what's—"

"No, it's a valid question." He took another nibble of his sandwich and chewed thoughtfully. "Marie's super hungover. Last night she went on a bit of a tear."

"That's what beer's made for," I said glibly, then stuffed half of Sandwich #3 into my mouth, and choked. Harris cracked open one of my sodas and passed it to me. I gulped convulsively to clear my windpipe. Awesome.

"Marie made a fool of herself last night. I'm surprised Jules and Malika didn't mention it. She showed up at the Cake Shop already drunk and kept knocking 'em back. . . ."

"Jules gets paid to make a fool of herself. Probably didn't even notice. And Malika's too sweet to gossip."

"Trust me, they noticed," he said, staring down at his plate.

I wanted to run over and demand that Malika fill me in on every single thing that happened, but I just sat there gobbling my way through Sandwiches #3 and #4 and avoided looking at Harris.

When he spoke next, his voice was so quiet I almost missed it. "She also thinks I . . . like you."

I choked another time. "S—sorry?"

"Yeah."

I waited for him to say more. He didn't.

"Do you?"

Wow, I hadn't meant to really say it. Harris looked as surprised as I was.

"Uh, maybe," he said. "I mean, yes. I think she's right."

I was stunned—that I'd asked the question and that he'd responded so truthfully. I couldn't look at him, so I looked at Sandwich #5 and wondered if I could get away with going for #6. Eagle-eyed Harris would definitely make some kind of comment. At least I still had carrots left. Oh, god, why couldn't I stop eating? Especially at a time like this. Maybe I had parasites. Could you catch parasites from a dog bite?

"We've been together so long," Harris said, interrupting my panic attack. "Sometimes I don't remember what Marie and I have in common."

We'd never had a single personal conversation, and now he seemed determined to peel himself open like an onion during my half-hour lunch break. The only thing I could think of to say was: "From where I'm sitting, you two are lucky. I have trouble meeting guys I like enough to hang out with for more than five minutes."

"Right. You could have your pick of guys. I've seen them fall all over you after concerts."

"I'm shy," I said. "Or picky. Shy and ridiculously picky."

Harris leaned over and rested a warm hand on my torn fishnet-covered knee. He liked me. Holy crap. I wanted to jump him. But first I needed more meat! I got up to nab Sandwich #6 from the food table and heard Harris's phone ring. He answered it in a low voice, glancing up at me, then turned away. I caught a bit of his conversation: "Look, not now. Marie, I know— Oh, for— No! Can we talk about this later?"

I was too embarrassed to eavesdrop anymore, and I was still pissed with Jules, so I decided to avoid everyone by ducking into the swanky bathroom and locking the door. It was the size of a small living room and had a comfortable love seat.

Putting down my plate on a wicker table, I dunked a stack of paper towels in icy water and wrapped them around my neck like a scarf. Then I turned off the light, sank down on the sofa, and nibbled on my roast beef in the darkness.

My stomach didn't feel too good—all that meat was a shock to the system—but I just couldn't stop. By the time I was done, my world was spinning. I swung my feet onto the couch and lay as flat as possible, hoping it would help. What was up with my body? And what was up with *Harris*? Since I had no answers, I squeezed my eyes shut, pressed my hand to my unhappy tummy, and tried to stay calm.

CHAPTER 4

SOMEONE BANGED on the bathroom door, jolting me awake. Reluctantly, I removed my paper towel scarf and opened the door. Light flooded the room, making me wince. I caught my reflection in the mirror and realized there was a wet circle around the collar of my personally tailored black-and-hot-pink roller derby T-shirt, and all the bracelets had fallen to my wrist, uncovering the scar. I shoved them back up my arm. The stylist was going to murder me!

Spyke stood on the other side of the doorway, glaring. Oh, shit. How long had I been passed out? Long enough for the whole crew to finish lunch and get into position around the stage. Jules fiddled impatiently with her keyboard. Harris and Malika looked worried.

"Why was the light out?" Spyke demanded. "Are you high?"

"No!" Not again. "Sorry. I fell asleep."

Spyke sniffed. "Are you *dying*? Because you'd better be."

"Can I get back to you on that?" I held out my hand, indicating she should move and let me past.

Spyke stepped aside and waved toward the stage. "We're going to have to make up the lost time. I've got more important things to do than babysit rock stars."

Unbelievable. I'm as close as you can get to straightedge without

being religious about it. Just to irritate Spyke, I slouched my way over to the stage as slowly as possible.

The makeup artist scurried over with her loaded powder brush and a tube of lipstick. She instantly noticed the ring around my collar and shrieked like someone had stabbed her. "Wardrobe! Bring me another shirt! This one's soaked."

The stylist shook his head. "No can do. It's one of a kind, cut and sewn to Sam's exact measurements. She's tiny!" He glanced toward Spyke, unsure what to do.

"Come on, it's just a shirt," I said. "Give me something else and I'll change. Who cares what I'm wearing?" I didn't mean to insult the stylist, but I wanted to get this over with.

"You can't change clothes at a random point in the video," said Spyke.

"Let's try a blow dryer," suggested the makeup artist, already running for her supplies. She came back, unraveling an extension cord as she walked and aiming brutally hot air at my neck. Just what I needed.

Spyke flopped dramatically into a fold-up chair. After about two seconds under the blow dryer, I had sweat pouring down my face and back. I could feel pools forming under my arms, in my elbows, and behind my knees. Even my toes were sweating.

A wave of roast beef–flavored bile rose in my throat. Gross. I gagged once, then a second time. I barely managed to stop myself from tossing my sandwiches right there. No one else seemed to notice. They were all too busy being irritated by the delay.

It was like something broke inside my brain. I couldn't handle another second onstage. I jerked out of reach of the hair dryer and away from the pounding light. Immediately, I felt better.

"Is it dry?" asked Spyke.

"Not yet!" said the makeup artist.

"Then finish the job!" Spyke yelled.

The woman moved forward, heat ray aimed at my neck. I darted away, knowing that the cord could reach only so far.

"You're screwing everything up," said Jules, in her typically blunt manner.

"Stay out of this, okay?" A sudden impulse to lunge and tear her throat out was so strong that my body shook with the effort to control it. The last thing I wanted was to get in a serious fight with her. That would cause a lot more trouble than getting under the director's skin. "Look, I'm not in great shape today."

"No shit, Sherlock," said Jules.

"I think I should go home. Something really weird happened to me last night—"

"Oh, please, enlighten us all," Spyke broke in.

"A huge dog attacked me after the concert," I blurted out. "Maybe I caught rabies or some other kind of infection. I don't know. I went to the hospital this morning, and the doctor seemed to think it was just the flu, but I'm freaking out and can't stop eating."

"Maybe you *should* go home and rest," said Malika.

Her kindness hit harder than a punch to the solar plexus. My eyes filled with tears. Malika was ready to believe me—no questions asked. "Yeah. I'm sorry. I know this is really inconvenient."

"Damn right," griped Spyke.

Harris stared at his feet awkwardly. Vinnie grumbled and checked his phone.

My nausea surged. I clamped a hand over my mouth, tore across the room to the garbage can, and puked. Loudly. A collective gasp rose from the crew as my six sandwiches made a reappearance in the world. When it was over, I straightened and wiped my mouth delicately with a wad of napkins. I felt like I was burning up and wasn't sure if it was fever or humiliation.

"Ewwww," said Jules.

I shot her a warning look, grabbed my jacket off the back of a chair, and tried to throw Janis over my shoulder. Unfortunately, the case's latch wasn't properly shut, so she tumbled out. Harris dived and caught her before she hit the ground. I nodded my thanks at him, afraid to open my mouth. I couldn't imagine what he thought of me.

The stylist flapped his arms and hurried toward me. "The shirt! Sam, don't leave with it on!"

I yanked the shirt over my head and tossed it at him. Then I took off, wearing nothing but a red-and-pink bra under my jacket—my underwear was getting a lot of airtime lately. But in New York, people would think it was a fashion statement. Out in the hall, I pushed the elevator's DOWN button frantically.

What a mess! Maybe, if I just went back to sleep, when I woke up my life would be normal again. I was still standing there in a daze when Harris and Malika came running out to the hall.

"You okay?" asked Malika, handing me the shirt I'd worn to the studio.

"Please leave me alone," I said, sniffling as I pulled it over my head. I was not going to cry in front of Harris. Not. Going. To cry.

"We want to help," she said, touching my shoulder.

I hiccupped. "I'm n-not kidding, Mali. Something's wrong—I'm messed up in the head!"

"You're sick," she said.

"In the head."

"Not true. You're just tired and sick. Don't worry about the shoot. Vinnie'll deal with the fallout. Jules is bitching, but she always gets over it. And this video is the biggest thing that's ever happened to Spyke. She shouldn't talk to you like that."

"Thanks," I mumbled.

I blinked to push back the tears. The elevator doors opened. I rushed inside and jammed my thumb into the lobby button repeatedly, trying to hide my face in the corner. Just as the doors were closing, Harris jumped in with me.

Once we were alone, he clasped my elbow and pulled me into a hug. His hands slid beneath my shirt to the bare skin of my lower back. I shivered. He held me tightly against his chest. I sucked in a breath and let my head fill with his scent. His body was noticeably cooler than mine. After all these months, I'd finally gotten his attention, and was in no shape to handle it.

The doors opened at the lobby to a rush of people waiting to get on. I twisted and wriggled loose from Harris. Without glancing back, I left the building and jogged down the street toward a busy intersection to catch a cab.

When I got home, I felt a burst of energy. There was no way I'd be able to rest. I ran upstairs to drop off Janis, scrub off my makeup, and grab a bottle of water. Back out on the street minutes later with my bike, I pedaled east through Brooklyn's side streets, away from the snarl of traffic.

Almost instantly, my muscles sang, my nausea subsided, and my mood improved. No violent or inappropriate urges. The exercise really seemed to help. So I kept going and became a cycling *machine*. My goal was to make it out to a quieter area and find a nice park where I could hang out. By the time the sun began to set, I was in some Long Island suburban enclave with cookie-cutter housing complexes on all sides. This would have to do. I was alone except for the occasional SUV whizzing past with a soccer mom and her 2.7 kids.

I'd finished the last of my water an hour ago and wished I'd stopped to buy more at one of the markets that lined the busier streets. Turning a corner, I spied a sad old apple tree. It grew next to a field overrun by grass and shrubs that was doomed, from the sign posted in front, to become more box houses.

As good a place as any to take a break. I eased my leg over the crossbar. That's when I discovered just how sore I was and collapsed on the bristly grass. My thighs and calf muscles spasmed. The sky was a fiery orange red. Beautiful. I fingertip-drummed the rhythm to "Not Missing You" on my stomach and tried to forget about my aches and thirst.

A vintage 1970s half car, half pickup rounded the bend in the road. I gawked at its sleek black-and-white hood. The owner must've put in a lot of effort to keep that thing polished and running smoothly. It rolled to a halt a few feet away. The driver's-side door opened, and a familiar-looking guy got out. It was Marlon, Harris's buddy from art class.

Although his narrow face was set in a surly frown, he wasn't hard to look at. His light-brown skin, slightly pointy chin, and artistically tousled black hair made me think of a young Johnny Depp. He was wiry almost to the point of being thin, but he looked strong, and his painted-on jeans emphasized his muscles. He also had on a purple-and-green T-shirt and black high-tops with lavender laces.

In one hand, he held an economy pack of beef jerky. In the other, a big bottle of spring water. Water! My eyes automatically went from the bottle to his bicep, decorated with a dark-blue tattoo. As he got closer, I was able to make out that the drawing was a howling wolf's head.

I waited silently, figuring he'd explain why he'd pulled over. Instead, he tossed the snacks on the ground, dropped down beside them, and leaned back on his elbows to enjoy the sunset with me.

"The snacks are for you," he said after a moment.

There was nothing actively threatening about him. He wasn't encroaching on my personal space. Well, not exactly. He was three feet away. For some reason, he didn't seem as creepy as his brother, but the situation made me really nervous. How had he found me out here? What did he want?

He slid a pack of cigarettes out of his back pocket and lit one. The smoke tickled my nose and made me sneeze.

"Do you mind not blowing that in my face?" I said.

He shuffled a little farther over and turned his head to exhale, leaving untouched the water I so desperately craved and the dried meat. I glared at him. When he was finished, he ground the butt into the dirt.

"Did you follow me?"

"Yeah."

Again I waited for an explanation but didn't get one.

"Pretty nice view," he said, flicking his brown eyes in my direction. "My name's Marlon."

"I know. Harris told me."

"And I know who you are."

"Why are you stalking me?"

"I'm a fan," he said in an oddly flat way. He still made no effort to explain what he was doing way out here in the boonies, on this deserted stretch of road, at this exact moment.

"But what are you doing *here*?"

"I came to help."

Okay. I was stuck in the middle of nowhere with Mr. Mysterious. People always assumed they knew me based on an interview I'd given or a certain song's lyrics, but they didn't usually go this far. Suddenly, the gorgeous sunset felt like a blazing warning that it would be dark soon. I shook out my legs. The thought of getting back in the saddle was thoroughly unappealing. Then again, so was hanging out here with my Number One Fan. Apparently, Harris had terrible taste in friends.

But *Marlon* was the one who should leave—I'd found this tree first. Before I could say as much, he shot me a disarmingly crooked grin. I groaned.

"Okay, move along," I said. "I'm not interested in sharing my apple tree. I came out here to be alone."

"So it's *your* apple tree?"

He jumped up and picked a plump, low-hanging fruit, then bit into it with relish, as if he had no worries in the world. I watched him chew in disbelief. If my legs didn't hurt so much, I wouldn't be sitting here having this conversation at all. I'd be back on my bike, out of here. Leaning forward, I tried rubbing my leg muscles, hoping to ease the cramps.

He tossed the apple core aside, folded his arms behind his head, and shut his eyes. "Sam, I understand what you're going through. All the strange feelings and reactions."

"What the—?"

"You must be terrified."

I *was* scared. And I needed to get away from him. Now. Somehow my exhausted legs let me stand up, but then they wouldn't move another inch. My knees wobbled dangerously.

"Sit down. You can hardly stand. I'm not going to bite."

"Just go away! Why are you still here?"

"You're ridiculously warm, thirsty, and hungry . . . right? You feel like you could eat three cows—raw—and drink a swimming pool dry." He gestured toward the bottled water and the beef jerky on the ground. "Those will help."

My eyes narrowed. "I'm not stupid enough to eat your roofie-laced snacks."

"Do I look that evil?"

I shrugged. "Stalkers come in all shapes and sizes."

"Sam, I wouldn't even know where to get roofies. I was serious about the cows, by the way. Let your mind relax, and they'll start to look an awful lot like prey."

"Shut up."

He let out a soft hiss of air, as if I was testing his patience. Reaching over, he opened the package of beef jerky. The scent of salty meat triggered my extrasensitive nose. He nibbled on a piece, and my stomach growled loud enough to hear.

"Aren't you curious how I know these things about you?" asked Marlon, stuffing another sliver of dried meat into his mouth. He lifted the bag and shook it at me.

"Obviously you stole my chart from the hospital or paid those idiotic doctors to give it to you. Then followed me for hours. I could have you *arrested*."

"I didn't read your chart."

He didn't bother denying that he'd followed me, but he was lying about this? I crossed my arms and stared at him. "Right."

"I know it's hard trusting people when you're famous. I promise my interest in you has nothing to do with that."

Small talk clearly wasn't Marlon's strong suit. I rallied all my energy and did the robot over to my bike, stifling a groan when I stooped to pick it up. Every muscle in the lower half of my body was screaming. It took me a minute to attempt to swing my leg over the seat. And I yelped in pain when I did it.

"Wait it out," said Marlon. "Your muscles will be fine in an hour, if you eat and drink."

"Don't follow me, or I'll call the cops." I took out my cell and waved it in the air. Of course, I hadn't plugged it in last night, so it was stone dead. My mom and Vinnie had forced me to get one, but I hated the thought of being within everyone's reach 24/7, so I regularly "forgot" to charge it. My big plan was to ride just far enough away to be out of sight, then find somewhere to recover in peace. I shoved off with one aching foot.

"See you soon, Sam," Marlon said, waving.

CHAPTER 5

AS I PEDALED, my fears of Jerky Boy were quickly squashed by the sheer misery of forcing my legs to propel me forward. Up ahead there was a wooden construction fence blocking out a new subdivision. I could hide behind that.

Then I heard the thrum of Marlon's antique motor. The engine got louder as he got closer. Once we were neck and neck, he slowed down and kept pace. I didn't glance over and he didn't say anything, so we just traveled down the road together in silence.

It became painfully clear how much I was suffering. He pulled closer and leaned over to wag the water bottle out the passenger-side window. I swerved away, causing my front wheel to bob from side to side. Yanking the handlebars back into alignment almost made me do a face-plant. I wondered if I could pull some kind of kamikaze move and run him off the road.

When I glanced in his direction with a grin, he gunned the engine and pulled up out of range. He might be a psychopath, but he was smart. I'd read somewhere that real psychos don't act psycho—that's a myth. Their MO is to pass for normal so they can hunt prey more effectively. Marlon definitely wasn't going out of his way to act normal.

My legs couldn't take the abuse anymore. They stopped spinning

the pedals. I squeezed the brakes and tumbled onto a freshly cut lawn. My limbs were glued to the ground.

I lay there, staring up at the darkening sky as the engine died and Marlon's footsteps crunched across gravel. His keys jingled as he twirled them around a finger. He dropped the snacks next to me and took a seat on the grass.

I peered at the bottle of water. Its seal *appeared* to be intact, though he could figure out how to fake that. Poisoned water would be an awful way to die. I groaned. "Why are you doing this to me?"

"Look, Sam, I have plans tonight; but if you want to throw your bike in the back, I'll drive you to the city. We can even get you a burger on the way. There's a place that uses free-range beef just outside Garden City."

"Go away. *Please.*"

"I'm actually having dinner with my parents, who live close by," he went on, as if I hadn't spoken at all. "You could come there with me. But just say the word, and I'll take you back to Brooklyn."

"So you're admitting you know where I live?" I asked pitifully.

He scooped up a handful of pebbles and began to lob them onto the road.

"Give me one good reason it would be safe to get into your car."

"You don't really have any other choice. I saw your phone isn't working. I didn't bring mine, or else I'd let you use it."

"I'd rather die here than *help* you take me somewhere so you can cut me up into tiny pieces."

He snickered. "You're not ready to trust me right now. So why don't I take you to my parents' place? They can explain what's going on better than me. They've been through all of this, too."

"No way." *All of what?* I wondered.

"What could be safer than coming home to meet my parents?" he asked.

"Hmm. Pretty much anything? I have no clue who you are or what you want!"

He laughed. "You still think I'm a stalker? Come on. My folks are perfectly normal professors. You'd like them. Maybe you've even heard of them: Françoise and Pierre Lebrun."

Of course I had. They were in the New York news all the time: NYU activists who coordinated relief missions for the United Nations. They'd written a best-selling book about how business interests impacted the way we helped New Orleans after Katrina. My mom was obsessed with them. If this guy was related to *those* Lebruns, I'd eat my pink Chuck Taylors.

"You can't get more harmless than academics," he said.

"I bet you've never even met the real Lebruns."

"They've got a guest room."

"What, we'd show up and you'd be all, like, 'Hey, Mom and Dad, I want you to meet Sam Lee. She'll just nap for a bit before I drive her out to a secluded forest and kill her.'"

The flash of annoyance that crossed his face left me feeling anything but safe. I'd finally gotten under his skin. But all he did was lean back on the grass, close his eyes, and mutter, "Okay, your call, Sam."

The sky was bright blue where it met the horizon and pitch-black above us. After a few minutes, I caught myself dozing off. A terrible idea, but that's how exhausted and drained I was. I tried to wake myself up by moving a bit.

"How do you know so much about me?" I asked.

He opened one eye. "I have a talent for fading into the background."

I snorted. "Helps with your stalking hobby?"

"I find your scent fascinating."

"Eww. You've been close enough to smell me?"

"I can smell you from here."

I was about to say something rude when I inhaled deeply and realized I could smell him, too. His scent mingled with the trees and grass around us. Beneath the soapy top notes were citrus and a low, enticing musk. I exhaled, covered my nose with my sleeve, and stared at him. His eyes were closed again, so he didn't notice. He was relaxed, his chest rising and falling evenly.

That's when my gaze lit on his car keys, abandoned in the grass. My fingers inched toward the ring. I shot my hand out and nabbed the keys, then jumped to my feet. *Sucker.*

He bolted to a sitting position. I shoved him as hard as I could and careened toward the driver's door. As I grabbed the handle, Marlon started barreling toward me. I slid into the seat, slammed the door shut, and locked it.

Marlon flung himself at the windshield, pounding furiously. "I'm trying to help you!"

I stretched over to slam my fist down on the passenger-side lock—no electronic systems in this old girl. He roared, kicked a tire, and then punched the hood so hard the car rocked. He was stronger than he looked—he'd put a big dent in the metal. I bet he was going to regret that later.

Shoving his key into the ignition, I jammed the car into first gear and stomped on the accelerator. The tires squealed. I left

Marlon and my bike at the side of the road, engulfed in a cloud of dust.

It took two hours to get into the city. The traffic was oppressive. As if every tourist in the world had decided to visit at once. While I was stuck in the Battery Tunnel, I poked around in the glove box and found receipts from cafés and a bookstore called Words of Wonder that specialized in "The Unexplained, Occult, and Otherworldly." He'd bought a book called *Guide to Shifters* by Mariela Rojas.

The registration papers were there, too, and they listed a home on Long Island. Maybe he hadn't been lying about where his parents lived. But the El Camino was in his name, so there was no proof that Pierre and Françoise were his parents. I jotted down the address on a scrap of paper and shoved it into my pocket.

I drove to the Village and parked in a lot close to NYU. It seemed like a good place to leave his car. Then I bought myself a mammoth smoked meat sandwich—with extra meat—caught a cab back to Brooklyn, and limped up to my loft. The red light on my home phone was flashing, but I ignored it as I ate my meat and drank a jug of water.

Temporarily sated, I opened my laptop and looked up the phone number that went with the address in Marlon's car. The listed name was P. Lebrun. I grabbed the phone before I could convince myself it was a bad idea.

A woman answered. "Hello?"

"Um, hi, Ms. Lebrun?"

"Françoise."

"From NYU?"

"Yes, of course. May I help you?"

So Marlon hadn't been lying about that, either. I didn't know what to say.

"If you're a telemarketer, dear, please don't waste any more of your time."

"No, no . . . I'm not a . . . I know your son. Marlon. Kind of."

"That's good, because telemarketers are paid peanuts. Horrible job. I always try to convince them to unionize. It's the only way to get respect in the workforce, you know."

"Yeah, I guess." I took a deep breath. "Uh, Françoise, I wanted to let Marlon know I left his El Camino in the lot—"

"Marlon? He's just coming in the door. Hang on, I'll get him for you."

"No! Please don't do that. Can I give you a message? I have to run."

"Oh, certainly. What is it, dear?"

I told her where the car was. "It's paid up until tomorrow night. The keys are with the guard."

"Marlon loaned you his car?" asked Françoise.

"Uh, yeah."

"He never lets anyone drive it."

"Well, he let me," I said, then hung up. At least now he couldn't charge me with grand theft auto. I plodded into the kitchen. My numbers were blocked *and* unlisted, so he wouldn't be calling back.

I took out Janis, climbed into bed, and played through the rough patches in a new song called "Cry Little Soldiers" until my eyes shut.

My dreams melded together into one long, vivid horror-movie reel. I ran through dark streets. Terrified people screamed at me in pig Latin. Cars honked and sped up when they saw me coming. Drivers tossed garbage out their windows at me. Strong smells—half-eaten, rotting food, exhaust fumes, cheap perfume—were dizzying. Several times I felt compelled to stop and root out the source of a particular scent. The city was a cesspool. Stink compressed my lungs.

While I was sniffing a refreshing tree in a park, I almost got lynched by four toy poodles, who barked and lunged for my throat. All I wanted was to be left alone—unless someone had food. Almost no one did, not the kind I wanted. The scent of fear seeping from people's pores confused me. My nose and perspective were closer to the ground than they should've been, making the streets and side-walks and buildings a series of close-ups and bizarre angles. Then the sky cracked and rain pounded down, surrounding me in a cool, wet cocoon. The streets cleared of people. I raced home.

As I passed the third floor in my building, something made me stop. A terrier waited on the other side of the door. I could hear her snuffling at the crack underneath. Hoping to scare her, I lunged at the door and went nuts, scraping at the wood. She whimpered and backed away. I howled in victory and ran up to my place, slipped inside, and nudged the door shut. I ignored the agitated pounding of humans on the other side and crawled into bed.

Sometime after my absurdly realistic dream ended, a low, rumbling noise woke me. Still half asleep, I assumed it was the downstairs neighbors, getting back at me with some new and unusual torture. Or maybe it was the wolf from Central Park, hunting down its prey. . . .

My eyes shot open. I peered into the darkness at the foot of my platform bed but couldn't see much. The ladder had fallen off, and the bedding beneath me felt oddly lumpy. It looked like I'd been sleeping *on top* of the pillows and comforter in a kind of nest. I was also naked. Huh? I didn't remember putting on pajamas last night, but I generally wore them.

I pulled a sheet around me like a dress, jumped out of bed, and walked around the apartment, turning on all the lights. The place was empty. I was losing my mind. Maybe I had posttraumatic stress . . . or I *was* delusional. I wanted to call the police or the park rangers or *someone*, but that wouldn't go down any better than my visit to the hospital. And my mother would just start with a bunch of hippie psychology stuff. There really was no way to explain any of this without sounding completely insane. Plus, I was starving again.

Wallowing was *not* an option. I lifted the bed's ladder back into position. A ball of cottony fabric lay on the floor beneath it: my nightgown, torn to shreds. I shuddered, picked it up, and shook out what looked like mud and fur. I tossed the ruined nightgown into a garbage bag, then wiped up the dirty footprints all over the floor. Wait, were those dog prints?

Was there an actual dog in here? Now my dream world was bleeding into my waking life. Cleaning rag in hand, I followed the prints to the door. The rough wood floor on the other side didn't show any prints. I cleaned out there, anyway. Focusing on a concrete task helped me to stay calm. What I wanted to do was run screaming through the streets. *It was only a dream . . . unless the downstairs tenants and their dog were somehow inside my place?*

After I finished cleaning, I perched on the side of my tub and examined the scar on my arm with a magnifying glass. There wasn't much to see by now. I imagined an army of white blood cells rushing to the rescue at breakneck speed, the skin tissue knitting together to heal itself. Maybe I wasn't losing my mind at all. Maybe Dr. Alam was right: I was turning into a superhero.

Another surprise awaited me up in bed. Switching on the light, I saw twigs, grass, and clumps of moist soil scattered across the mattress. I inspected the mess with a sinking feeling. After changing the sheets, I lay down and closed my eyes, just for a minute. . . .

It was midafternoon by the time I crawled out of bed again. My eyes were puffy, and my head ached. Between chugs from a pitcher of tap water, I nibbled on dry crackers. The fridge was now officially empty, except for condiments and a head of lettuce rotting into soup.

I ditched the lettuce, plugged in my cell, and checked all my messages, knowing my mom must be waiting to hear from me. Sure enough, she was about to send out a search party. Vinnie'd also called to yell at me that we needed to reschedule the video shoot. The third-floor neighbors were demanding I put down my violent dog. The only pet I'd ever owned was a guinea pig in third grade whose death had convinced me I never wanted to go through that again. The message would've been funny if it wasn't so bizarre: "This is a one-dog building, and Zoe was here first. One dog, you hear? We refuse to live anyplace where Zoe feels unsafe."

Jules had called, too, demanding to know "exactly what is up your butt?" Malika had checked in around noon. Her voice was heavy with concern, which made me feel guilty—but not enough to call her back right away. Mostly because I had no clue what I could possibly say that would relieve her worries. The final message was a surprise: Harris. He confessed he'd pried my number out of Malika and wanted to know if I felt well enough to grab a beer at the Cake Shop later on.

I'd never be able to face any of these people until I'd eaten, so I grabbed my wallet and jogged the six blocks to our local supermarket. I felt as if I could run forever and added that to the new list of things that made no sense about my life.

CHAPTER 6

ENTERING THE STORE, I knew someone was frying sausages and zoned in on the sample booth, where I pretended to have a hard time choosing between the six varieties. After allowing me to taste each of them twice, the sample woman began to cluck like an angry hen. So I tossed a few packages in my cart and hurried away.

My cart filled up with a huge barbecued chicken, turkey bacon, three sirloin steaks, two pounds of ground beef, an economy-sized package of pork chops, and a rack of lamb. I tossed in a bag of oranges and a dozen cans of frozen lemonade—not because I particularly wanted them, but because the vitamin C might counteract the gout I would surely get from my new all-meat-all-the-time diet.

As I unloaded everything at the register, a skinny brunette who seemed to be on a macrobiotic diet got in line behind me. She started to pile her greens on the counter, frowning judgmentally at my mountain of meat, then she looked up at me and gasped. "You're in that band! I saw you in an ad for PETA! Aren't you vegetarian?"

I blushed and began to babble: "Oh, yeah, that's me. This meat is for a . . . friend's barbecue. I agreed to . . . uh . . . bring the protein. Ewww! Animal flesh! Right?"

The woman nodded once, then tossed her sprouts and fresh vegetables onto the counter and hunted around in her handbag.

"Someone else is bringing the condiments," I said, cringing inside as I continued to blather. "Ketchup, mayo, herbs, marinade, and stuff. Another person's on salads . . . starches. You know."

The woman's head bobbed, but she wouldn't meet my eyes.

A barbecue in October? I really needed to work on my lying skills.

I paid as fast as I could, grabbed my bags, and marched out the automatic doors. My cheeks were pink, but my head was held high.

Too famished to wait until I got home, I sat behind a tree in the park across the street and dipped into one of the bags to find my barbecued chicken. I ripped off a juicy leg. Just my luck: the moment I shoved it into my watering mouth, the woman who'd been behind me in line walked past. She raised an "I knew it!" eyebrow, whipped out her phone, and snapped a few pics.

I bared my teeth and leered greasily. That photo was totally going viral. No way to stop it. At least eating meat wasn't illegal. I tossed the clean bone into a garbage can and dug into a wing as I crossed the park. I found myself turning down my mom's street. The smell of brewing coffee wafted out the apartment door as I unlocked it. My mother might have a loose grip on reality herself, but she made the world's best espresso.

Betty Mitchell, aka Mom, was reading the local news section of the *Times* at the kitchen table. Her long sandy-brown hair was tied up in a messy loop on top of her head. Her jeans and smock were smeared with dabs and squirts of every imaginable color. Her painting clothes should be framed as works of art in their own right.

She glanced up. "Sammy! I didn't know you were around today, sweetie."

"Wasn't supposed to be."

"What's wrong?"

I ignored her question and swooped down to plant a kiss on her cheek.

"How's it going?" I asked.

She sighed. "You want a happy answer or the truth?"

"Happy," I said without hesitation. Mom was always losing it about something. She had what I called "excessive empathy." When she shoved the paper away, I guessed that she'd been about to rant about the news. "Thanks. I could use a little more happy right now."

"Ahh. Okay, I won't pry." She paused anyway, hoping I'd elaborate. I didn't. "Well, then. I'm working on my portrait gallery for the big show tomorrow."

I'd been so preoccupied, I'd forgotten about her show.

She pointed at a new row of paintings leaning against the wall—all bright slashes and dabs of color that hinted at animal-like figures. In recent years she'd developed a name for herself as a painter of pets. Mom took the portraiture very seriously and didn't work from photos. She made several appointments with her "clients" so she could capture the true essence of Little Fido or Dottie. What I loved about her art was that it was such an interpretive process. Sometimes you couldn't even tell her images were based on cats and dogs. Once I'd accused her of simply painting abstracts, and she hadn't denied it, just raised an eyebrow and murmured something about "auras." The show she was preparing for was a featured exhibit at Woofstock, a dog owners' convention in Toronto that she drove to every year.

"Looks great," I said, shoving my bags in her fridge, then taking a seat across the table. "Those remind me a little of graffiti murals."

"They're one of my inspirations," she said, clearly pleased I'd figured that out. "To get into dogs' heads, I need to reflect their natural environments. Where do they spend a lot of time in the city? Alleys!"

So Mom was skulking in alleyways these days? Perfect. If I told her about my recent dreams and adventures, she'd be afraid of every shadow.

"Making espresso?" I asked, glancing pointedly at the percolator on the stove.

"It's almost ready," she said.

I licked my lips greedily. "Caffeine deprived."

She stood up and took two hand-painted cups from a cupboard above the sink. Mine had a picture of a toad snapping up a fly. Mom's handiwork. "Is Vinnie working you too hard?" she asked.

"No more than usual. Just having wicked food cravings."

My mother's face froze and her cheeks turned a splotchy red that meant she was in shock. This was why I didn't tell her things. She jumped to horrific conclusions.

"Mom, god, no! I'm not pregnant!"

She smiled. Then tensed again. "Are you sick?"

"My body just seems to, uh, need certain foods right now."

"Are you anemic?"

"Maybe. And I'm running a bit of a fever. The doctor says I'll be fine."

"Well, I'm glad you saw a doctor. Sounds like some kind of infection."

"Maybe."

She took a container of cream from the fridge and set it down in front of me, along with sugar and little spoons. "You know, I wasn't much older than you are now when I had you. . . ."

"Change of subject! Please!"

"Okay." She patted her hair anxiously, but only succeeded in making it messier. "Sam, you need to be serious about these things.

It takes only one careless moment. Or, in my case, a night of incredible, reckless, passionate—"

"Thanks for the mental image."

My mom had told me that my dad was the most beautiful man she'd ever met, and they had absolutely nothing in common. They got married and had me, and when he told her he was leaving, she realized she was okay with it. Neither of them was cut out for marriage. So she raised me on her own. Mom had a few boyfriends over the years, but she truly did seem happier on her own. I couldn't blame her. I'd kept my father's last name because Sam Lee was cooler than Sam Mitchell; and if it sounded a bit like Stan Lee, that was a bonus.

As she filled our cups with scalding black liquid, I leaned forward to inhale the deliciousness. Then I slammed mine back.

"What was the bad thing you didn't tell me before?" I asked, feeling a little guilty for shutting her down. And somehow it seemed like the safest topic. "I'm ready now."

My mom refilled my cup. "Well, when you came in, I was reading about these girl gang muggings that have been happening downtown."

She picked up the newspaper and passed it to me. I skimmed the article and flashed back to the news clip I'd seen in the hospital lobby. "It's disturbing," I agreed.

She nodded. "All this violence! I don't know why it seems so much worse that teen girls are doing these things. . . . I guess it just doesn't happen often. There've been three attacks in the past two days."

"Do they know who's doing it?"

"Not yet. It's just horrible. They dress up like dogs, and there are bite marks and scratches on all the victims."

It sounded eerily familiar. Scanning the article didn't give me any new info. There was a blurry black-and-white photo of two teens taken by another security camera. It looked as if one of them wore a glove shaped like a paw, complete with vicious claws.

"Anyway," Mom said, "there's more bad news. I just got a call from the folks at Silicon Systems on your first floor. Their ceiling's leaking. Your problem tenants have probably flooded their bathtub again."

"I'm going to rip their heads off!"

Her eyes widened. "Don't overreact, Sammy. The Silicon guys went down to the basement and shut the water off as soon as they realized what was happening, and I've called a plumber."

"Is there damage?"

"Nothing major."

"How about the guy on the second floor?"

"Not answering, so I'm not sure yet."

I forced myself to breathe calmly and poured myself a third cup of espresso, which I drank in two seconds. When I helped myself to the last dregs in the percolator, my mother's eyebrows communed with her hairline.

"Wow, I guess I'll make more for myself."

"Oops, sorry," I said. "We're gonna have to replace the drywall on the ceilings, too."

She started to clear the table. "It's just in their storage room. Not a big rush. You know, Sam, the best gift you can give yourself is to listen to your body. If you're craving certain things, like caffeine, or feeling really irritable and stressed, it's nature's way of telling you something's wrong. . . ."

I flopped back into my seat, wondering why she'd stopped

herself midlecture. Normally, she could drone on and on about how I needed to make healthier choices for my body. Then I figured it out. She'd opened the fridge to put away the cream and my grocery bags had slumped over, allowing her a glimpse inside. Uh-oh.

"Sam, um, is there anything else you want to tell me?"

"My body needs more protein."

"But I never thought you'd be a meat-eater again."

"You make it sound like I've become a cannibal. Aren't you glad you don't have to make tofu and beans for me anymore?"

"Sure, but—"

I looked at the clock on her wall. "Oh! Gotta jet."

"Okay, Sammy. Be careful out there."

I extracted my bags from the fridge. "Hey, do you know how to cook a rack of lamb?"

Frowning, she took something out of a drawer. A meat thermometer. She pressed it into my hand and told me to heat the lamb to 140 degrees. "What kind of rub will you use?"

Spices hadn't even occurred to me. She gave me a head of garlic and some rosemary. I accepted the bounty and sprinted for the door.

"Feel better!" she hollered after me.

"I'm fine!" I yelled back as I hurried out. I really needed someone to talk to, but it wasn't going to be my mother.

I took out a drumstick and gnawed on it as I walked down the street. I'd made it half a block when someone yanked my arm—hard—forcing me to turn around and sending my chicken leg flying through the air. My first thought was it must be the vegetarian police! I dropped my bags to free up my other arm. The four self-defense classes I'd taken were about to become seriously useful . . . if I could remember them.

I recognized my attacker. She was the girl I'd seen with Marlon's brother after The Puffs' concert. Ponytail Girl. Behind her was her friend, Freckles, wearing a very realistic wolf's paw. Just like the girl in the newspaper article!

"Let go of me!" I hollered.

"Shut up!" Ponytail Girl spat, still gripping my arm.

She wore long sleeves and jeans, but I could see that dark hair peeked out around her neck, wrists, and ankles. So thick I'd call it fur. I'm not a shaving fanatic or anything—I'm more of a "be comfortable with your natural state" girl. But I gaped at the thick fur.

"Stay away from him," she growled.

"Who?"

"Don't play dumb," said Freckles. "This is for your own good."

Then Freckles high-kicked me in the chest, knocking me on my ass, and they ran off.

Winded and thoroughly confused, I clambered to my feet, picked up my bags, and trudged home. I couldn't stop myself from checking around corners for lurking girls.

What guy did they want me to stay away from? Harris? Had Marie sent the world's weirdest girl gang to warn me off her man? Or could it be Marlon? And why were they wearing costumes? Were they really costumes? I had a sinking feeling again. That fur looked awfully real.

Back in my apartment, I locked the place up tight and heated up the oven. My hands were shaking as I fumbled with the raw, bloody piece of some poor sheep's rib cage and shoved it in the oven, despite an almost irresistible desire to just put the thing in my mouth and suck on it. Ugh. I was grossing myself out. Since it would take an hour to cook, I tossed a package of sausages into a pan and fried those up, too. Six of them slid down my throat nice and smooth. The water was still turned off in the building, but I squeezed out enough to make a pitcher of sugary lemonade.

I considered going downstairs to confront the tenants but didn't trust myself. I was about to pull out Janis for a practice session when my cell rang.

"Hello?" My caller was playing the Commodores in the background. Nice.

"Uh, hang on." The music lowered. "Sam? It's Harris. Feeling better?"

"Sure," I said, and realized I wasn't lying. Had all the meat helped?

"I was worried. You well enough to go out for a beer?"

An image of Marie gazing at him adoringly jabbed my conscience. Arrgh. What to do?

"Okay," I said, after waiting too long. "You don't have plans with Marie?"

"I'm free."

Free as in no plans, or no girlfriend? "What's Marie up to tonight?" I couldn't stop.

"Dunno. We're taking a break. From our relationship."

"Wow." When did that happen?

"Yeah."

"You guys always seemed so happy."

"Well, we weren't."

Awkward silence . . .

"Wanna meet at the Cake Shop around seven?" he asked. "They've got new work by Jordan on the walls."

Jordan Watanabe was the comic scene's current It Boy. He and Harris shared a studio. Going there tonight meant we'd run into their friends. My hanging out with Harris in public so soon after his breakup was probably not a good idea. I thought of those crazy girls this afternoon. Scratch that. Definitely not a good idea.

"Sure," I heard myself saying.

We hung up, and I played Janis until the rack of lamb was ready. If I was going to sit around the Cake Shop for a few hours and not fidget like a junkie, I should eat more. And so I did—more sausages, half the rack of ribs, and another piece of chicken for dessert.

It wasn't a date with Harris. Um. Right.

I wasn't exactly a mastermind of the flirting arts, but I knew I couldn't show up looking like a sweaty monster, in sneakers and saggy yoga pants. I agonized for five minutes, then pulled on my favorite jeans and a sexy green tasseled top that brought out my hazel eyes, and added mascara, black eyeliner, and lip gloss. A thin jacket would keep me warm enough these days. At the last second, I tossed all the remaining lamb ribs and sausages in a plastic bag and stowed it in my purse. A girl never knew when she might need a little meat.

I pulled on a cap to hide my face and took the subway to the Lower East Side, then wandered a handful of blocks over to the Cake Shop. Two blocks away, I noticed a weird bookstore nestled between an art supply shop and a clothing boutique. Words of Wonder. I knew that name—from the receipt in Marlon's glove box! Peering through the front window at stacks and stacks of new and used books, I could see that ancient tomes had been heaped carelessly on top of magazines and loose sheets of paper. The owner didn't seem to worry about making any sales. That always amazed me in this city where rent was so high.

I yanked open the door, causing an old-fashioned bell to jingle above it. When I stepped inside, I was barraged by Nas rapping about hip-hop being dead. The song was so loud and at odds with the store's ambiance that it threw me off, and I tripped over a pile of books on the floor.

As I bent to straighten the books, I could feel the young guy behind the counter watching. When I glanced at him, he jutted his chin as a greeting. He looked a few years older than me. Quirky cute face, in a Gael García Bernal kind of way. He wore an oversize red T-shirt with a Fight the Power fist on it that brought out the golden tones in his skin. He tilted his head and let his eyes sweep from my feet all the way up to my face. Then his nose twitched and he squinted, as if he was surprised by something.

As I stood, I caught a glimpse of his laptop screen and saw that he was designing a website for the bookstore.

"Can I help you?" he asked. His voice had a certain lilt to it—South American, maybe? His irises were dark brown and abnormally large.

"Just browsing," I said. "A friend recommended your store."

He came out from behind the counter and stood close to me—too close, frankly. The guy was very tall and wide: a bit of a linebacker. He sucked in a deep breath and exhaled hard enough to make my hair move. His nose twitched again. I tried to take a step back, but the aisle was too cramped.

"Dude, did you just smell me?" I snapped.

"Of course not." His tone and his slow grin told me he was making fun of me. "The meat in your purse, on the other hand . . ."

"Excuse me?"

His eyes scanned my body again. Either he was flirting very badly or looking for a tail. I almost bolted right then.

"You *do* smell fantastic, though," he said. "Musky and powerful and healthy. Too many girls cover up their natural scent with perfume. I'm glad you don't. And you look quite normal. Interesting . . . So you want a book on shape-shifters?"

"No. I mean . . . Yes. Shape-shifters. How did you—"

"Follow me. I know every book in this place."

He started down an aisle. How could he guess exactly the book I wanted when I wasn't sure myself? And how could anyone possibly make sense of this mess? Shelves climbed up to the ceiling and appeared to have been randomly filled. Books overflowed into piles on the floor. Some shelves were two books deep. Handwritten signs identified roughly how things were sorted. By the time I made it over to him, I'd seen a few intriguing categories: mythological creatures, hexes and charms, gods and idols. . . .

He pulled out *Guide to Shifters*, carried it over to the counter, and punched the cover price into the register without bothering to show it to me. I spotted *How to Pick a Mate: Survival Tips for the Hairy and Fabulous*, and I couldn't resist, so I handed that over as well.

"Are these books for real?" I asked.

He didn't respond, just shook his head as if I was being an idiot.

"Okay, Chatty Chris. You own this store?"

"Nah. My *abuelita* does, but I fill in for her sometimes. That'll be thirty-four nineteen. Ten percent discount since you're a Mary."

He obviously meant the infamous virgin. I refused to acknowledge the quip and pulled out two twenties. He already had my change in his hand, as well as a stiff off-white business card that had only an e-mail address and DANIEL ROJAS, KNOWLEDGE KEEPER, WORDS OF WONDER. I accepted both, then turned to leave. Daniel's casual "Looking forward to the next time, sugar" sounded like a promise.

CHAPTER 7

AT FIVE AFTER SEVEN, I entered the Cake Shop. It was packed. Jordan's comics-inspired panels dominated all the walls. Harris was at a corner table, talking to some guy and already nursing a half-finished pint of beer. Right above their heads was Jordan's painting of Homer Simpson wearing one of Marge's dresses and a tall blue wig.

I passed the counter where they sold old vinyl and CDs by local bands. Someone had hung a Cream Puffs poster advertising our monthly jam in the basement space—which was happening tomorrow. It was the poster with Jules hanging her tongue out Kiss-style, Malika bouncing so her skirt flipped up and showed a flash of white lace, and me playing and glancing shyly down at my bass. It felt like a huge neon sign pointing right at me. A half-dozen heads turned to gawk as I slipped into the seat across from Harris. A fangirl tried to wave me down, but I flashed her a distant smile and turned away. Harris's friend realized he might be intruding, said hello to me, then disappeared.

Pretending not to notice when Harris leaned across the table for a hello hug, I tossed my bag between our feet and made a big show of craning my neck to take in a painting of Spider-Man and the Green Hornet making out.

"Jordan's pretty twisted," I said. "In a good way."

Harris looked disappointed, but he turned his gaze to the walls. "We met in high school—hung out at lunch drawing superheroes. Used to be roommates, too."

I nodded, because I already knew both of those things through the grapevine. "Before you moved in with Marie?"

"Right." He drained the last of his pint. "And now that we've split, I'm back at Jordan's place, crashing on the couch."

"Ahh." So they broke up last night?

"Want a beer?"

"Uh, okay." Except that they wouldn't serve me because they knew I was underage.

He nodded but didn't stand up. Instead, he rested his forearms on the table and bent over his own glass, bringing our faces very close. His breath smelled like beer. I could have leaned over and kissed the tip of his nose. It was hard not to stare at the curve of his full lips, which quirked upward slightly, and the way his soft brown curls moved whenever he did. He looked especially delicious tonight in his distressed-cotton T-shirt with a picture of Hopey and Maggie from *Love and Rockets* on it. I'm such a comic nerd, and Hopey's one of my idols—the original tough girl, flawed and real.

"Feeling okay?" he asked.

"I'm fine," I said, slumping backward as much as possible. It was warm in the Cake Shop, which wasn't helping me any. A raunch-heavy track from a few years ago came on—the one where Peaches does a nasty duet with old Iggy Pop. I could've used something to help me cool down, not get me more worked up.

"You were really out of it yesterday," said Harris.

"Ugh. It was pretty awful."

He nodded sympathetically. I wondered if Jules and Malika would accept my excuses that easily when I eventually got around to calling them. Doubtful.

"I'm actually superthirsty," I said, not wanting to talk about it. I could hardly believe he was still interested in me after that disaster.

He jumped up. "Oh, sorry. I'll go order."

Then he strode off, forgetting to ask what kind I wanted. I hated most beer. I was all about rum and Coke, if I was going to drink at all. Which was, like, never. Oh, well. If he'd asked, I would have preferred iced tea and one of their cupcakes. I'd noticed a red velvet with hot-pink icing and cream cheese filling on the way in. Maybe Harris was used to having a girlfriend whose favorite food was common knowledge. Or maybe he'd done his research and would surprise me.

Up at the bar, he ordered from a bleach-blond Ke$ha wannabe wearing a pink baby doll dress. They talked as she poured two pints of beer. Gross. After he'd moved away, she saw where he was headed and her smile faded. I couldn't tell whether she was upset because I was underage or because I wasn't Marie. It was a relief when Harris blocked her view.

He'd brought me a light ale, which meant he had no clue what I drank. I picked up a list of bands that would be playing in the basement and fiddled with it.

He gestured with a thumb toward the bar. "Tanis and I are old friends."

"You probably can't go anywhere downtown without bumping into someone who knows your work."

His smirk acknowledged the truth of my statement. "I guess it's the same for you?"

I whistled. "Oh, yeah."

He picked up his beer and drained it all at once. Either the guy could handle his alcohol—or he was on a crash course. If I finished this pint I'd be halfway under the table. I had a well-honed technique to avoid getting drunk, which was to wet my lips for hours on end. I took a healthy swallow to get it started and made sure I didn't grimace at the taste. The beer tasted especially bitter.

"Tanis knows Marie?" I guessed.

"Yes."

So the evening wasn't off to a roaring start, thanks to my big mouth and overactive conscience. And this gross beer . . . I shoved it away.

"We were fighting a lot," he said. "Marie and me."

I leaned forward. "That sucks."

He nodded. His eyes dropped to my mouth, and he moved closer. Was he going to kiss me right here in front of all these people? I wanted him to, maybe. No, I didn't. Tanis would start a riot. I sipped my beer, just to create a barrier between our lips.

"You barely know me," I whispered around the glass.

"I know you, Sam. We've worked together."

"But you just—"

He reached over and touched the back of my left hand, which currently had a death grip on the edge of the table. It let go. He began to rub my palm with his thumb, which was pleasantly cool against my feverish skin. I sat there, enjoying the sensation and looking down at our hands. My fingers had thick calluses from the strings, and his were long and thin—an artist's fingers. My heart was pounding like it wanted to break through my ribs. He was single. Marie wasn't in the picture. It really did change everything.

I yanked my hand away from Harris's and brought my beer in

for another sip, only to discover it was empty. Oh, no. Where did all that beer go?

"We've got an audience," I said, flicking my gaze toward Tanis, who was still throwing eye darts at me between filling orders.

Harris gritted his teeth. "She's not the only one. Bad place to meet. It's crawling with people who know Marie."

"And The Cream Puffs," I said, nodding at the poster.

"You hungry?" he asked.

"I could go for a snack," I said—the understatement of the year.

"What do you feel like?"

"How about sushi? There's a place nearby."

He stood and pulled on a black jacket, then picked up his canvas bag and dug out a cardboard envelope. "I forgot. This is for you."

As I followed him out the door, dodging the mass of people who'd come in since we arrived, I peeked in the envelope to find the completed sketch he'd done of me at the video shoot. Seen through his eyes, I looked composed and beautiful: focused on playing my bass, a tiny bit fragile but confident in my own skin.

It had begun to rain, and the wind was blowing angrily. I tucked the drawing into my purse next to the bag of meat. Harris had wisely brought an umbrella. We huddled together under it as we splashed through the dirty streets of lower Manhattan. Drivers took advantage of the quiet traffic to whip around corners at top speed, spraying water onto the sidewalks. And onto us. Puddles overflowed and formed rivers in the gutters, carrying garbage and debris along.

The heavy rain muted the lights and drummed a free jazz rhythm on parked cars and trash cans that would've made a musician like Ornette Coleman jealous. The dreamy chaos bought me a little time before I had to deal with Harris again. This emotional stuff was scarier to me than all my other recent encounters.

Beside me, Harris shivered. My hand reached out and wrapped around his, clasping the umbrella's handle. Too bad I couldn't will my excess body heat to flow into him. He winked at me. I winked back.

"We could always skip the food and go straight to your place," he suggested, wiggling his eyebrows.

I actually giggled. "Forget it. You're rebounding hard. And I'm not *that* easy. Plus, I really am hungry. Famished."

"Aww," he pouted. "I thought you were all about sex, drugs, and rock 'n' roll."

I pinched his arm, making him yelp.

We tumbled into the restaurant. Unfortunately, every single table was taken. Not only that, but a soggy lineup nearly blocked the door from opening. I felt equally guilty and relieved when the owner recognized me and ushered us through to a private booth with a RESERVED sign on it. I'm no Beyoncé, but I'm enough of a local celebrity to reap the benefits sometimes.

The smell of all that fish made me drool. I surreptitiously scooped up a napkin, wiped my mouth, and then reached for the owner's arm before she could bustle back to her duties. Without waiting to find out what Harris wanted, I pointed at a picture on the menu's first page: a heaping pile of sashimi arranged on a large bamboo boat, enough for two people and their dog. "Bring me one of these!"

"Just for you?" asked the owner.

I started to nod but noticed Harris's expression and changed my order to a more appropriate one-person serving. Then I had to wait impatiently while he took his sweet time poring over the menu, only to pick out chicken teriyaki with vegetables, pork dumplings, and steamed rice. Not a single piece of raw fish in the whole deal. He also asked for warm sake. Even though I was happy with green tea, the owner came back and presented each of us with a thimble-sized cup, then poured the wine.

Harris raised his sake for a tiny toast. "To new experiences. And new *friends*."

The way he said it left no doubt which friend he wanted to experience. He reached over and clasped my hand again. My fingers twitched, and I almost pulled away. With my free hand, I took the tiniest sip of the deceptively mild rice wine. Even those few drops burned their way down. I was in trouble.

"So, what's going on with *Dream Rage* these days?" I asked.

His comic's plotline seemed like firmer ground than what the hell we were doing on a date, and Harris was happy to chatter away while we waited for our food. He explained that the last issue's ghostly apparition—which floated around the main character at night, taunting and insulting him—was supposed to be a physical manifestation of low self-esteem and neuroses. I could relate. The final artwork for the next issue was due to the publisher on Wednesday, and Harris was worried because he was behind schedule and wanted it to be absolutely perfect. It inspired me to hear someone else take his art as seriously as I took mine.

While he talked, he tossed back more sake. I wet my lips a few times. He didn't notice my drink was still full and tried to top it up each time he poured more for himself. When the food arrived, my cup was stone-cold and overflowing, and my stomach was on the verge of a revolt. I'd already considered—and reluctantly rejected—grabbing food from the plate of a slow eater sitting near us.

My small sashimi boat was digested in about thirty seconds. Using chopsticks, I hauled three slices of fish into my mouth at a time. I didn't pause for a breath until the final piece was sliding down my trap.

When I glanced up from the empty plate, I saw Harris was watching me again. Uh-oh. And I was *still* fiercely hungry. Screw it. I reached across the table and popped a piece of his teriyaki chicken into my maw.

"That was *fast*," he said.

"I told you I was hungry."

"You haven't touched your salad . . . or the rice."

"I'm cutting back on carbs."

I forked up a few unappreciated bites of lettuce.

He didn't respond, but attempted to add more liquid to his sake cup and realized the bottle was empty. A few feet away, the chef tossed Kobe beef onto the hibachi. I desperately wanted some. Then I remembered I'd brought my own meat pack. I couldn't pull it out here, while Harris was daintily pecking at his salad and drinking soup, so I excused myself and headed for the bathroom.

Locked inside a stall, I removed a garlicky piece of lamb, trying not to think about how unhygienic the entire situation was, and started gnawing away. Mmm. So good.

The bathroom door swung open. Two women entered and began to talk at the mirror.

"What's that smell?" said one.

I froze, rib hovering between my teeth.

"Garlic?" asked the other.

I tore off the remaining meat and shoved the bone back into the bag, wincing as the plastic crinkled, then tried to hold the zip seal closed until the two women left so it wouldn't smell so strongly.

As the door shut, I heard one of them hiss: "Someone was *eating* in the stall."

"Gross!"

When had I been reduced to a nut job who ate flesh in public bathrooms? But I couldn't stop. I fished out a sausage and bit off the end, hoping it didn't reek as much as the lamb. A few people came and went as I tucked into the rest of the meat, but no one else cracked any comments.

I thought about shoving my Ziploc of bones into the container for "feminine products," but the bin was too full. Instead, I tucked it back into the bottom of my purse and flushed the toilet for show. At the mirror, I washed my hands, picked a piece of lamb gristle out of my teeth, and freshened my pink lip gloss. Judging by Harris's face when I returned to our table, I'd been gone a little too long.

"There was a line," I said lamely.

He glanced at the women's room—where there wasn't a single person waiting at the door, damn it—but nodded politely.

"Been trying to get the waitress's attention," he said. "Wouldn't mind another bottle of sake." His glazed eyes said he'd had enough.

My cup was still full. I gulped down the contents. I needed it. Harris frowned. He'd been hoping I'd offer it to him. It must be weird to hang out with a stranger after dating the same woman for eight years. Maybe that's why he was drinking so much. Or did he miss Marie?

The server was running around manically, delivering meals and taking orders, but when I stood up and waved, she rushed over. I asked for the bill before Harris could order another round.

"I was waiting for fifteen minutes," grumbled Harris.

"I've got magic powers," I said. "They can be helpful in certain situations."

"Maybe *I* should try being famous."

I smiled ruefully. "Not always as much fun as you think. Trust me."

"But you get to jump lines. And you've got groupies."

"I'm not exactly the hook-up type, in case you haven't noticed."

"I've noticed," Harris said, licking his lips.

The server distracted me from staring at his mouth by returning with the bill. I won a brief argument about who was going to pay by snatching the bill and holding it behind my back. Harris teasingly threatened to come after it. He staggered to his feet and almost pitched right over. He had to clutch the chair. I took that opportunity to hand some money to the waitress. Harris shook his head in mock anger, then barreled out of the restaurant.

He'd already hailed a cab when I made it outside. I jumped in beside him, grateful to get out of the rain. Harris told the driver to head for Williamsburg. Jordan lived in the East Village. As we were speeding through wet streets, he turned to me. "We're going to your place."

Did he expect an invite upstairs? "Uh, how about we head to your place, then I'll keep going to Brooklyn?"

"No way. Ladies first."

I told the driver my address. Harris inched closer until our thighs were touching. He rested a hand on my knee. It was so warm, I could feel it through my jeans. Rebound Boy *was* hoping to get lucky. As we rode over the illuminated bridge, I glanced at Harris. In the flashes of light, he looked gentle and tired.

My heart ached a little for him. Breakups were hard. I'd only really been through one. I dated a sound techie for about six months. We weren't right for each other. All he talked about was the music industry, which was a total snooze if you lived and breathed it. Still, when we broke up, I felt like I'd been flattened by one of Wile E. Coyote's giant anvils and basically hid in my apartment and lost myself in music for a week.

The cab pulled to the curb in front of my building. I got out more money to pay.

" 'T'son me," slurred Harris. "You paid for dinnerrr!"

"No, I—"

"Sam, please!"

"Okay, thanks." I gave him a quick hug and opened the taxi door, but couldn't get rid of him that easily.

"Wait!" Harris blocked the door with his foot, sprawled sideways, and slapped cash into the driver's hand before clambering out of the car.

The cab pulled away. We were alone.

CHAPTER 8

I YAWNED AND STRETCHED exaggeratedly. "It was really nice hanging out, but I'm going to bed now."

He swayed in my general direction. "But we've hardly had a chance to talk. It's early, and this is the city that never sleeps."

"Brooklyn?" I joked.

He gave me a playful shove. "New York . . . Invite me up?"

I sighed and shook my head.

He grabbed my waist and pulled me against him. His lips were suddenly pressed to mine, parting and nibbling. Heat rose up my knees, through my abdomen, and settled in my chest. I closed my eyes and inhaled the scent of Harris Wall. Beneath a layer of alcohol and a surprisingly sexy cologne was a deep male musk that smelled so unbelievably good. He would probably taste amazing.

What the—? My eyes flew open. I jerked back. I could just make out the bounce of a pulse under the thin skin of his neck. I moved farther away.

"This isn't happening," I mumbled.

"It's been a long time since I've kissed anyone other than Marie," he said. "But, wow!"

He craned forward. His mouth lowered again.

"Watch yourself, Harris. She might eat you." A guy was standing in the shadows next to my front door. *Marlon.* His hair was flat, and his clothes were soaked through from the rain, leaving nothing about his body to the imagination. I squinted at the quote in pale blue letters on his black shirt: "In wildness is the preservation of the world." A Thoreau fan.

"Marlon? Why are you spying on us?" asked Harris.

"I'm waiting," said Marlon. "For Sam. And, like I said, I'd be careful if I were you. She really was on the verge of ripping your throat out."

"Get lost," I snarled, remembering the intoxicatingly sweet smell of Harris's blood.

"I just stopped by to thank you for returning my car in one piece."

"What are you guys talking about?" asked Harris. "Sam borrowed your El Camino?"

"More like stole it," said Marlon.

I rolled my eyes.

"I thought you guys didn't know each other," Harris said.

"He *doesn't* know me!" I shouted. "But he followed me when I went for a bike ride and wouldn't leave me alone. I jumped in his car to get away!"

"Oh," said Harris, frowning. "You were really following her? Not cool, man."

"I needed to talk to her. Alone."

"Anything you have to tell Sam can be said in front of me," Harris declared.

Great. I was now officially in the middle of a duel.

"Okay, then." Marlon looked at me. "First, I'm returning your bike." He pointed toward the wall—sure enough, there stood my somewhat wet but otherwise intact trusty pink steed. "Second, a monster really *did* chew on your arm while you were riding in Central Park that night. Third, I can help you understand the changes you're going through. Fourth, if you don't let me help, you're going to do something you really regret. Soon."

"You rode through the park at night?" asked Harris, squinting at me. "That's not very safe."

I bared my teeth at both of them. Marlon knew about the dog attack? How? The last thing I wanted was not one but *two* guys telling me what was good for me. I already had a mother, a manager, and bandmates for that.

"Go home, Harris," said Marlon. "She's about to get wild."

"Hey!" said Harris. "There's no need—"

"Leave." Marlon wasn't joking anymore.

Hurt and confusion flashed across Harris's face.

"Listen," I said to Marlon, "this is *my* home. I appreciate you returning my bike, but if you don't go away, I'll call the cops."

"Fine. I'll leave, too. You know how to find me when you need answers. Trust me, Harris; don't go upstairs tonight. I'm serious. Besides, you reek of Marie."

"It's not news that Harris *just* broke up with Marie," I said.

"Yeah, well, breaking up isn't the only thing they've been doing today."

I leaned over and sniffed the air near Harris's shoulder. Sure enough, there was a sour note beneath the musk. Was that Marie? Jules was always saying breakup sex was fantastic. Had they really . . . ? One fact was for sure, Harris's split was too recent for me to get involved.

Fed up with everything, I took out my cell phone and waved it around in the air. "That's it, Marlon. I'm counting to three. You'd better be gone by the time I'm done."

Marlon opened his mouth to argue, then clamped it shut again.

I began to count. "One . . ."

"You should leave, dude," said Harris.

"Two . . ."

"Why don't you tell him about your bag of *meat*?" muttered Marlon, quietly enough so Harris couldn't hear.

And how did he know about my stash?

". . . Three!"

I pushed 911 on my phone, but before I hit CALL, Marlon jammed his hands into his pockets and stalked away. His back was rigid. The muscles in his shoulders and upper arms stood out like cords beneath his wet T-shirt.

"That lamb shank had way too much garlic!" he called back to me.

I refused to give him the satisfaction of a response but couldn't help thinking about the guy in Words of Wonder, who'd been sniffing me earlier this evening. My life was getting off-the-charts weird.

I slipped the phone back into my bag, next to the books. Why the hell had I bought them, anyhow? Stupid, stupid, stupid. My life was not a Wolverine comic.

Harris was still gaping and scratching his head. There was no way to salvage this night. "Do rock stars have to deal with this kind of thing all the time?" he asked.

"More than you know."

"I swear he's never acted like that around me before." Harris sighed. He didn't seem drunk anymore, only sad. "This wasn't a very good date, was it?"

"Not Hall of Fame level, no. Maybe we're just moving too quickly. I wouldn't blame you for needing a little time to get over your relationship."

He scuffed a piece of crumbling pavement with one shoe. "Sam, I really like you and hope you give me another chance. But I promise I didn't break up with Marie because of that. It's something I've—she and I have needed to do for a while."

I looked him in the eyes, and I believed him.

"Thanks for the picture," I said.

Before anything could destroy the moment, I gave him a peck on the cheek, then hurried inside.

When I got upstairs, a lumpy manila envelope was stuck to my apartment door with industrial tape. I tore it off and went straight for the kitchen, where I gnawed happily on a piece of barbequed chicken. It was a crazy relief to be by myself.

Once I had some food in me, I opened the envelope to find an invoice from the plumber my mother had called to fix the leak, a decomposing rag in a plastic bag, and a note saying he'd identified the cloth as being the source of the blockage. It wasn't the bathtub. The rag was flushed down the toilet. I tossed it on the floor. Come on! Really? Who flushes a *piece of cloth* down their toilet? At least this time I had evidence of the tenants' malevolence that I could take with me to court.

I sat down on the couch with Janis and started picking. The picking morphed into actual playing, which led to a productive practice session. By changing a single chord in the refrain and lengthening the intro slightly, the crescendo in "Dirty Street" got the chance to build a little higher and then swoop down. It would sound awesome when we tried it live.

In a much better mood, I foolishly decided I was strong enough to handle e-mail. After deleting three messages from Jules that began whiny and ended rude, I changed my mind. But I still read one more from Vinnie: Are you trying to ruin this band? CHECK THIS LINK!!!! Now you HAVE to go on The Wanda Show! HAVE TO!

He'd been trying to get me on Wanda Kalamata's talk show for the past six months. Wanda was this artsy comedian who'd snagged a daytime TV slot and interviewed New Yorkers who piqued her interest. She'd mentioned casually in an article that she was a big Puffs fan and would love to have me on her show. She could help us reach beyond a teen audience, but she terrified me. She was notorious for taking people to task on television. I clicked on the link and discovered the dreaded photo of me eating chicken in the park—and, crap, there was actually grease dripping down my chin! The caption on Wanda's website read: "Call PETA police, NYC, cuz Sam 'Veggie Girl' Lee is back on flesh in a serious way." I clicked the browser shut a bit too hard, which was better than smashing the whole damn computer. The entire world was apparently out to get me.

A few minutes of deep breathing allowed me to get back to fiddling with samples for "Dirty Street," inspired by sounds of the city partying at night. I'd collected background noises for weeks. When I finally stopped for a break, I called Malika. It was almost one, but she'd still be up.

Sure enough she brushed off my "Sorry for calling so late." She also brushed off my apology for the shoot.

"I'm just glad you called. I saw that *awful* photo on Wanda's site. God! What's wrong with people? How are you feeling?"

"Better." To convince her, I told her about my ride to Long

Island, my disaster of a date with Harris, and how Marlon showed up at the end with my bike. By the time I was done, she was guffawing.

"I'm glad someone finds my misery funny."

"Oh, *poor* Sam," she drawled. "Two hot guys are making asses of themselves over you."

I snorted.

"You've been lusting after Harris forever," she said. "Now he's available. Who cares if the breakup's messy?"

"Yeah, but—"

"And if it doesn't work, you've got a new guy waiting in the wings."

"Mali!" Something made me hold back from telling her about my stranger experiences with Marlon.

"Well, he's got your attention, doesn't he?"

"Not in a nice way!"

"So he wants to do naughty, naughty things to you."

I laughed at her sexy voice and tried to shut down the mind movie she'd created. We hung up shortly after that, and I went back to working on the song. My goal was to mimic the slow click of high heels with Malika's steady *ticka-ticka* drumbeat, then add the screech of car brakes, horns, heavy dance club bass, and the distant whine of police sirens. Digital percussion and a synthesizer would have to approximate real-life instruments for now. By looping the urban noises on top of one another, I created a wall of sound that Jules's voice could dance over, hitting high and low notes, and imitating the cacophony of wild, drunken night chatter.

The next time I stood up to stretch, it was three in the morning, and my body demanded food and exercise. I did jumping jacks for a few minutes, then tucked into the last piece of chicken and half a pitcher of lemonade. That's when I noticed the big old window above my stove was wide-open. What the hell? That's why the apartment was cooler than normal. And I wasn't sweating like a dog. But who'd opened it, and when?

I climbed onto the counter and wedged the pane shut with a mop handle. When I'd bought the building, all the windows were sealed shut with layers and layers of paint; and after getting central air installed, I'd never bothered to unseal most of them. Like this one. It would take a crowbar and a lot of strength to crack that window open from the outside. Plus, my place was high off the ground.

I started to panic. Could someone jump from the fire escape that ran up this side of the building to the six-inch window ledge? If he lost his footing and fell to the street, he'd be a pancake. There were plenty of desperate people in the city, but it was hard to believe the average criminal would go through all that trouble to rob me. There were much easier targets.

A more logical explanation was that my mother had come over to let in the plumber and opened the window for some reason. Fumes?

It was really hard to convince my brain that having a full-blown panic attack wasn't helpful. More than anything, I wanted to dash over to my mom's place and huddle in her guest room. But my mom was leaving for her show this morning, and I wasn't ready to unleash all her worries.

I changed into pajamas, grabbed *How to Pick a Mate*, and climbed up to bed. I flipped on the lamp and almost had a heart attack. Marlon was lying there with his arms folded behind his head, looking completely relaxed.

"Nice book." He grinned as he looked at the cover.

I threw it over the side of the bed and opened my mouth to scream, but before any noise could come out, he'd jumped across the bed and clamped a hand over my lips. I'd barely seen him move.

My body began to shake. I wasn't sure if I was more angry or scared. I struggled to get loose, tearing my pajamas. He was strong. Really strong. My rage took over. How *dare* he break into my apartment! How *dare* he make me feel unsafe in my own bed! A growl tore from my throat. Flailing randomly, my fist made satisfying contact with his chin—then I kneed him hard in the gut. He squeezed my arms against my sides so I couldn't move at all.

"Sam," he hissed, "I'm not here to hurt you."

I cursed into his hand. My head flipped from side to side, like a fish on a hook, but he didn't let go. I channeled all my fury into my eyes.

"Sam, calm down. Please. You're going to hurt yourself."

I opened my mouth enough to chomp down on his palm and draw blood. A salty taste filled my mouth. He yelped. I ripped at his shirt and arms, feeling fabric and flesh give way. I didn't care how much damage I did; all I could think about was my freedom. I catapulted away, panting, but couldn't get off the loft bed because he was blocking the way down.

Marlon gripped his bleeding arms. "Sam, please don't scream, okay? Whatever you do, don't scream. No one can see this."

I shook my head and felt hair moving on my cheeks. *Hair? What the*— I touched my face and gasped. There was fur. On my forehead. On my neck, too. There was hair everywhere! And my fingertips ended in claws, not nails. Oh, shit. I began to whimper.

"Guess surprising you up here wasn't the best plan. Sorry. I actually fell asleep listening to your music. I just really needed to talk to you."

"How long have you been up here?" I demanded. My voice sounded strange, like it came out as a series of barks.

"Awhile. I'm really sorry for breaking in."

"You're sorry?" I wasn't shouting. I was too confused. What was happening to me?

"Sam, you don't have to go through this alone."

I crawled toward him. "Get out of my way."

He hesitated, then moved aside.

Swinging over the loft's edge, I jumped down and ran to the bathroom. In the mirror, a ghastly beast stared back at me. My face was covered in dark fur. When I yanked at the hair on my chin, it hurt!

Running back to the base of my bed, I shrieked: "I am a monster!"

He nodded. "You were bitten by a werewolf, Sam. You're turning into one yourself."

My brain stopped functioning. I closed my eyes. When I opened them, Marlon was hanging over the side of my bed, looking concerned. My hands were still paws. My face was still hairy. Clammy sweat broke out beneath my fur. My *fur*.

"I know it seems insane," he said.

"Because it is!" I yelled—but my words still sounded more like barks. My fur *moved* whenever I did.

He didn't respond. I realized Marlon hadn't fought back . . . and he looked totally miserable. He didn't care that I'd scratched him. It seemed like he didn't want it to be true any more than I did.

I sat down in the middle of the floor and dropped my head into my claws. I was a wolf girl. Half wolf, half human? Whatever. Fully freak show.

Somehow sitting there helped me calm down a little. As soon as I did, my paws began to change back into hands. My skin felt weird and itchy. It was like an elastic band was being stretched tight and then, suddenly, loosened. Over and over. Everything was intensely painful for a moment as the fur appeared to get sucked back into my follicles. Then my body was normal again, right down to the peeling black nail polish I'd applied a week ago. And all I was wearing was the tattered remnants of my pajamas. I jumped up, yanked the sheet off my bed, and wrapped myself in it.

"Take some more breaths and relax," said Marlon. His voice was reassuring, like a cat's purr. "Your body will always want to shift when you feel threatened, but you'll learn how to control that."

"How do you know all this?"

"You can guess."

"You think you're a werewolf?"

"I don't *think* I'm a werewolf, Sam. I *am* a werewolf."

In front of my eyes, his human shape began to waver and change. . . .

"Stop!" I yelled. "Please, stop. I can't deal with any of this."

His body stopped changing, and he just sat on the bed, watching. Did this explain everything that'd been happening to me? But . . . if I allowed myself to believe in werewolves, what did that mean? Suddenly, an endless number of ideas became possible. Enough to fill every shelf in Words of Wonder. What else lurked in our world, disguised as human?

"Zombies?"

Marlon stared down at me. "What?"

"Do they exist?"

"Probably. How should I know?"

"Fairies, vampires, witches . . . what about them?"

"I'm not an expert on the world's supernatural underbelly."

"So you're saying there *is* one?"

"Who do you think I am—Batman? I'm not keeping tabs on Gotham City."

"I don't know *who* you are." All my previous assumptions about him were changing. He wasn't a fan or a stalker. But it would almost be easier to accept that he was a superhero than to believe that both of us were werewolves.

Marlon tilted his head, sniffed once, and then a second time. He glanced toward the kitchen, lunged forward, and descended from the bed in one fluid movement. In the next instant he was standing on my counter, inspecting the edges of the windowpane I'd barred earlier.

"Someone else was here," he said. "You need to come talk to my parents. Now."

"I'm not going anywhere with you."

"You stubborn wolf." Marlon reached up and gave the mop handle a good yank to make sure it was jammed in there. I noticed the claw marks on his arms were already healing. He hopped down to the floor, picked up a pen on the table, and jotted a number on a scrap of paper. "But it's not a bad idea for you to rest. Call me when you need me. I won't be far away."

"That's not very comforting."

"It should be."

I slammed the door behind him. Not that it made me feel any safer.

CHAPTER 9

BACK IN BED, I stared up at the dark skylight. It felt like hours before I drifted off, and I woke up again almost instantly. I shook myself, hopped up onto all fours, and leapt off the bed. As I prowled around the apartment, I smelled under furniture and in the corners. There was a strange, furry scent around the kitchen windowpane—I could pick it up now. Through the floorboards, I heard Zoe running around, barking up at me. Her *yap-yap-yap*ping was so irritating that I had to silence her. Immediately. I hurled myself at my door until it opened.

When I lunged at the apartment door downstairs, it opened easily. Unlocked. A brief, furious standoff ended when I swung a claw at Zoe's head. She scrambled back to cower beneath a chair. I clamped my jaws down on her foreleg and shook. Eventually, she stopped whimpering.

I ran down to the ground floor, licking my lips. The front door was propped open. Outside, the cool night air cleared my brain. Marlon was sitting across the street in his car. When he saw me, he sat up with a jerk and reached for the door handle. I barked, warning him away. He held up his hands for a truce. I passed Zoe's humans skulking in the shadows. They smelled like smoke. And prey.

There was a scuffling noise behind me. I twisted in time to see

Marlon bearing down on me, holding a blanket. I sprinted away. He caught up with me, tossed the blanket over my head, and pulled me into his arms.

"It's okay, Sam," he whispered, holding me tight. "Relax. I've got you."

"Keep your animal on a leash, asshole!" the guy from downstairs yelled at us.

"Sorry. She got away from me," said Marlon. He kept a solid grip on me, and the blanket, as he moved us toward his car. I didn't resist, just slid inside and slumped in the seat. My body changed back to human form, and I found myself buck naked. I clutched the blanket around my shoulders and peeked out the window. My neighbors had finished their joint and gone inside, which meant they'd found Zoe by now. . . .

"I don't want to be a monster," I moaned.

"That's your choice," said Marlon. "You're different now, but whether you're a monster is up to you."

"You still want me to meet your famous parents?"

"Definitely. They can help, I promise. I'll run upstairs and get you some clothes."

I glanced at the clock on the dashboard. "We're going now, at five in the morning?"

He waved off my concern. "My family's pretty much nocturnal. We don't sleep for long periods at a time, even during the day, unless we're exhausted or sick."

"Okay, then . . . let's go."

"Great. They're looking forward to meeting you," he said.

"You've already told them about me?"

"It's not every day a new female enters our lives."

"A what?"

"Female lycan—lycanthrope, shape-shifter, skin-walker, werewolf, animal spirit. Take your pick. Whatever you want to call yourself."

He waited for me to mull that over.

"So, what do you call *yourself*?" I asked.

"Marlon Lebrun." He held out a hand for me to shake. "Nice to meetcha."

I smiled despite myself and pumped his hand. "Samantha Mitchell Lee. And you can't go get me clothes, because wolf me didn't stop to grab my keys."

He looked at me thoughtfully. "Did you lock your apartment door?"

I shook my head.

"No problem, then."

I rested my forehead against the window, listening to the driver's door open and close. He jogged across the street, pushed all the buttons on the intercom, and got lucky. One of my sucker tenants buzzed him in. He disappeared inside.

Marlon came running out ten minutes later, looking rattled. He passed me my canvas bag, quickly started the car—glancing anxiously back at the building as if he expected someone to come running after him—and pulled away from the curb.

"What exactly did you do to your neighbors' pet?" he asked. "That woman just chased me down the stairs with a soup spoon, accusing my *dog* of attempted murder."

I shook my head grimly. "I hope she's okay. I'll offer to pay the vet bills."

As he maneuvered through dark, quiet streets, I opened my bag and found a matching sports bra and undies, loose green skirt,

T-shirt printed to look like the top half of a tuxedo, and my favorite black hoodie. He'd also brought my flip flops, keys, wallet, and cell phone. I should've felt completely creeped out at the thought of him poking around my stuff, but I was too numb.

"I didn't get you anything fancy," he said.

"This is fine." I wrangled with my clothing beneath the blanket. After years of touring in a bus, I'd gotten pretty good at changing in moving vehicles. I was just glad I wasn't naked anymore. Or furry.

I tossed the blanket aside, suddenly much too hot, and relived the sensation of Zoe's leg bones cracking between my jaws. I felt queasy. Marlon glanced over but didn't say anything. I was grateful for that and struggled to calm down. He got onto the highway and retraced my bike route out to Long Island.

The smell of the cleaning products and oils that Marlon used to pamper the car settled around me. Fixing up an old classic rather than buying the most recent model appealed to me. But I'd never wanted the hassle of a car in the city. That's why I stuck to cabs, public transit, and my bike.

Soon, we were in the sprawling suburbs.

"Why did you pick an El Camino?" I asked. "I mean, why not a muscle car if you're into vintage. A T-bird or something?"

"It's easier to lug around bikes, or a kayak, or climbing gear."

The sporty lifestyle seemed at odds with his hairstyle and clothes. After the past few days, though, I understood the urge to use your muscles. I waited for him to elaborate, but apparently he didn't love the sound of his own voice. He also didn't expect me to entertain him. It was surprisingly comfortable to lapse into silence. I yawned and shut my eyes.

Marlon turned off the highway. I sat up and looked around, but all I could see was darkness. "I should probably prepare you," he said. "It's, um, been a long time since I brought a girl home. And my family has this thing where they say whatever's on their mind the second it occurs to them."

It was tempting to ask exactly *how* long it'd been since he'd had a girlfriend, but considering I'd mentally accused him of being a psychopath a couple days ago, I couldn't bring myself to do that. "No one could be worse than my mom," I muttered. "It's like she can read my mind."

"Is she a seer?" he asked.

"What's that?"

"They can channel others' emotions and thoughts."

I snorted. "Well, if she is, her powers work only on animals. And daughters."

He glanced at me. "Technically, you're both now."

Crap. My brain still couldn't handle it. My thoughts drifted back to the subject of Marlon's exes. What would his type be . . . Hipster? Punk? Intellectual activist, like his parents? Sporty babe who kayaked and rock climbed? Nothing fit.

He pulled onto a residential road. We passed a subdivision surrounded by green space and full of rich people who didn't want to live in the dirty city. But he didn't turn into the complex—he kept going up a densely wooded lane into a state park. About a mile later, he veered right, up a gravel driveway lined with trees. No streetlights pierced the intense darkness, unheard of in the city. Above us, I could see stars. Full constellations!

"Here's the family place," Marlon said, stopping in a random spot beneath a giant pine tree and cutting the engine.

I gaped. "You live here?"

"Nah. I've got an apartment near Washington Square."

"How big is their land?"

"Sixteen acres. The plot just feels bigger because it's next to a state park. No one's totally sure where the property lines lie."

This place could easily hold a housing development . . . or three. For an instant, I pictured a pimply fourteen-year-old Marlon with braces and perfectly spiked hair exploring this massive forest.

I peered through the trees and could see an old two-story stone-and-log house. A few lights were on.

"Ready to meet the monsters?" he joked.

"Are they . . . ?" I couldn't bring myself to say it.

"Are they what? Lycans? Yes, the whole family."

Meeting a guy's parents was stressful under any conditions. The Lebruns were best-selling authors, academics, *and* werewolves.

"That day on my bike, you told me they were normal professors."

"Oh, right. Well, they're pretty normal to me. And I didn't think you were exactly open to hearing the whole truth yet."

I crossed my arms. "So I was right not to trust you."

Marlon reached into the glove compartment, grabbed an open pack of cigarettes, and shook one out. He lit it, took a few deep drags, then stubbed the butt in the ashtray, exhaling white smoke into the chilly air.

We got out and crossed a long patch of grass to the house's stone front steps. A porch light turned on before we were close.

The door flew open, and the Lebrun family tumbled through the doorway as if they'd been waiting for us. I wondered if Marlon had called them when he was in my apartment. His brother was dressed in designer jeans and a black shirt with fiery-red Chinese characters stitched down both sides of his chest that meant "strength and power" (I'd studied a little Cantonese in high school because of my dad). Dark hair curled around his ears. His face was wider than Marlon's, with a square Superman jaw. He was larger and more muscular in general. When our eyes met, his raked up and down my body. I blushed, annoying myself.

"You're not deformed," Marlon's brother remarked.

What the hell?

"No, she isn't," said Marlon with an edge in his voice.

Their father stepped closer. He looked like a professor: a slim, elegant man with dark-brown skin, short gray hair, and horn-rimmed glasses, dressed in a button-down flannel shirt and beige corduroys. His wife hovered excitedly by his side. She was much shorter and slightly plump, with pale skin, tawny eyes, and flyaway chestnut hair shot through with a single strand of white at her forehead. As I peered at her, her nose twitched, and her head tilted upward. She gave Marlon a judgmental look.

"Smoking again?" she asked.

She could smell the smoke on him from that far away?

"He thinks it makes him cool," said his dad. "It doesn't."

"How cool will it be when he gets lung cancer?" asked his mom.

"Werewolves don't *get* cancer," said Marlon.

"Seriously?" I asked. "Wow."

"Our cells metabolize too quickly," he explained. "Sam, these are my parents: Françoise and Pierre. And this is my *baby* brother, Owen."

"Hey." I waved awkwardly, fighting the urge to turn and run— fast and far, without looking back. It felt an awful lot like I was onstage, standing in the spotlight. Owen snickered at my discomfort. Françoise stepped forward with arms outstretched. She looked safe enough, but I inched back. I wanted these people to like me.

Were werewolves technically *people*? I had no one else to turn to. But I was afraid of what I was about to learn.

"I'm glad you agreed to visit," said Françoise. She spoke calmly, as if I were a skittish animal, and she didn't try to touch me again.

"Welcome, Sam," said Pierre, offering his hand. I accepted it gingerly. He had a very energetic shake. I pulled away as soon as possible.

"As you can imagine, I'm very excited to meet another female," Françoise went on. Then, without any warning, she leapt forward, grabbed me, and enveloped me in a big hug. When she let go, she continued to clasp my elbow, as if she knew I was tempted to bolt.

"You're the first fully changed female any of us has met," said Pierre. "Other than my wife, of course."

"Oh," I said.

"You're rare," said Marlon.

"Extremely rare," Owen added.

"Something to do with the infection process," said Françoise. "Women's bodies fight the transformation. Some of us have such a terrible time—"

"They die," interrupted Owen. "Most females. Violently. Or else they're hideously deformed."

If only Owen wasn't staring at me so hard, I might not have felt quite so skittish.

"Stop crowding her, guys," said Marlon, shooing them all away. Once they'd backed up, I could breathe normally again. "She was turned less than three days ago. She's got boundary issues. Or maybe you're all so ancient you don't remember that."

"We're not *that* old, Marlon," said his father, chuckling.

"You're right," said Françoise. "Sorry about the hug, Sam. And holding your arm."

"Her hair's bristling," said Owen.

I patted the hair on my head self-consciously—it felt fine to me.

"If she had a tail right now, it would be curled between her legs," Owen went on.

"It *has* been quite a while since we were in your shoes, Sam," said Pierre.

"I've never been in them." Owen snickered again.

"Forgive us—*all* of us," said Pierre, shooting a warning glance at his younger son. "We're just extremely pleased to meet you."

"Let's go inside for a cup of tea," suggested Françoise. "Soothes the wild beast."

"Not as much as scotch," muttered Pierre, heading for the front door.

The four of them entered before me, then turned around en masse to watch my expression as I stepped inside. I gawked. Their house was like a museum. Every inch of wall space was covered with paintings, from the baroque to the abstract. There were statues, too. Mostly busts. A small soapstone carving of a man transforming into a wolf transfixed me. The living room had floor-to-ceiling shelves arranged neatly with books and crafts from around the world. Some of the stuff looked *really* old. Where had it all come from?

As we walked down a hall, Marlon said: "My parents travel a lot and always bring home something new."

"I research local artists' cooperatives," said Françoise, "and buy directly to support the cultural economy."

We passed a very, very old bronze helmet. I paused to examine it. "This looks Roman."

"That one is," said Marlon, nodding.

Passing through a wide semicircular archway, we entered their dining room, which was dominated by a long, antique wooden table covered in gashes and indents where heavy plates and silverware had worn it down. An entire wall of windows—open to let in cool air—overlooked the woods. Shadowy trees and bushes stooped toward the house like nosy old men.

"The temperature thing," I said. "Why do I feel better when it's cold?"

"Lycans run a few degrees warmer than humans," said Françoise. "Dogs are more comfortable when it's chilly, too. Your body is still figuring it out."

"Summer in the city is a bitch," said Owen, throwing himself into a chair. It scraped across the floor. He obviously expected someone else to handle making the tea. Marlon disappeared through a door on the other side of the room—presumably the kitchen—while Françoise and Pierre sat down at either end of the table. That left an open seat beside Owen, and two directly across from him facing the window. I chose one with a view outside.

"They say the first werewolf was created by a woman in Japan," said Françoise. "Her husband was a cruel man who beat her and bullied everyone in their town into submission. One day she just snapped and cursed him to become the impulsive, violent beast he was in his heart. The next full moon, it happened. That story is one of the reasons lycanthropy is considered the ultimate manifestation of inner rage."

"But it's just one of the myths," said Pierre. "It might be true—who knows? There are so many others to pick from. No one knows who our first ancestors really were. Some cultures believe all people have animal spirits. Others say werewolves are a super-race created to obliterate normal, weaker mortals—to thin the herd, if you will.

Our family has made it our mission to sift through the oldest stories and sort out possible facts from fiction."

"We do know certain things," added Françoise, leaning forward on her elbows. "The way people are turned, for instance."

Pierre glanced at his wife. She nodded.

"Did Marlon tell you how Françoise and I became werewolves?" he asked.

I shook my head.

"Didn't have time!" called out Marlon from behind the kitchen door.

Françoise looked at me. "If it's all right, Sam, Pierre and I will share our story."

"Okay." I shrugged. What could be worse than what I'd already been through?

Marlon entered the room carrying a tray laden with a silver teapot service, five china teacups, butter cookies, and a bowl of homemade beef jerky. He set it on the table. Before he'd even sat down, his family had pounced on the meat. They were stuffing hand-fuls into their mouths. I averted my eyes. For once I wasn't hungry. I was surrounded by an entire *family* of werewolves.

Still chewing, his mother poured tea into the china cups. Her movements were delicate. As I added milk and sugar to mine, I couldn't help thinking: *I have met the monster, and she is me.*

I took a gulp. Heat burned all the way down my throat, but a lovely floral bouquet bloomed in my mouth.

I cradled my cup to my chest. The warmth was reassuring and made me feel stronger. Across from me, Owen folded his hands behind his head, leaned back on two chair legs, and put his feet up on the table. He was looking forward to his parents telling their story.

CHAPTER 10

"I AM THE SEVENTH SON OF a seventh son," said Pierre. "There's a long-standing belief that such men become werewolves on the first full moon after their twenty-fifth birthdays. Seventh daughters of seventh daughters are fated to become witches at the same age—they come into incredible power."

Owen muttered something about his father being a windbag and snatched another handful of jerky. Pierre ignored him.

"When I was a child, my parents moved to New York from a small town in France," said Pierre. "I was never made aware of the legend . . . until it was too late. I've since learned that the other people in my parents' town were deathly afraid of me and forced my parents into exile."

"His first change happened while we were graduate students," continued Françoise, "working in the Cambodian rice fields outside Phnom Penh. We were doing a work-study placement with an aid organization, helping local people tend their fields and gain self-sufficiency in production and export."

"We refused to be separated," said Pierre. "Not even for a month."

"I wasn't supposed to be on that particular trip," Françoise admitted. "They needed only Pierre's expertise."

Pierre went on. "She came along because she was writing her dissertation and could do that anywhere. We had Marlon—he was just a toddler—so they stayed behind at the house we rented while I went out for daily hikes to inspect crops and speak with local experts. One day, it was sunset before I realized how far I'd wandered—how long I would have to walk to get home. That night, the full moon almost filled the sky."

"He transformed all alone in a remote rice field," Françoise told me.

Pierre nodded. "I was twenty-five. And didn't have the self-control to stay away from my wife and son. In wolf form, I covered the miles in minutes. Françoise woke up when she heard a scratching sound at the door. The moment she opened it, I lunged for her—"

"He almost ripped my throat out. I barely managed to smash him over the head with a lamp, grab Marlon, and run into the bathroom," she said. "He almost killed me . . . *would have* killed me." Her hands shook.

"Thank god the door was strong enough to keep me out," said Pierre. "Seeing her helpless and frantic fueled my hunger. My human judgment was obliterated—as it often was in those early days."

"You love giving in to the wolf, Father," said Owen. "Admit that it feels great."

Pierre ignored Owen again.

"I turned later that same night," said Françoise. "And joined him on the hunt." She shuddered at the memory.

What had they done?

"The desire to feed was unrelenting in those first few months," said Pierre. "Sam, I don't know how you've kept your control."

I thought of Zoe. "I . . . Well, I haven't. Not really."

"It took every ounce of my willpower to pass as human for any length of time. Françoise and I both slipped. More than once."

"I almost ate my neighbor's dog!" I blurted out.

"I killed someone, Sam," said Françoise.

"He attacked you with a pitchfork first," noted Pierre.

"Because we were slaughtering his cow. Only four cattle stood between his family and starvation. He was defending them from a monster."

"He would have killed us both," said Pierre, reaching for her hand. She nodded slowly, allowing him to twine his fingers through hers.

"When we came back to New York, we sent Marlon over to my mother for a few months," said Pierre. "Told her we'd both caught malaria. It was the only way we could think of to keep him safe. He was so tiny. Only three years old. I just wish we hadn't been so hasty to bring him home."

I desperately wanted to hear how Marlon had been turned. And Owen, too. But their parents fell silent.

Owen looked at them and then at me. "You're worried she'll run away if you tell her about me and Marlon? She's a wolf now, too. She survived the change. She'd better learn how to handle it."

"She's a *werewolf*," said Marlon. "Not a wolf, asshole. You know there's a difference. And it takes time to adjust."

"Oh, yeah," said Owen. "She has to adjust to being nearly indestructible, as powerful as three humans, having supersenses—it's just awful."

"She could have died," said Marlon. "Or killed someone."

Their mother broke in. "Your humanity will always be part of you, Sam."

"Your human side makes you weak," said Owen.

"You're wrong," said his father.

"Owen was born half wolf," explained Françoise. "So the wolf side has always been dominant in him."

"It's not his inner wolf that's been causing trouble lately," grumbled Marlon.

Owen stood up and slammed his palms on the table. "What's your problem!?"

"You. Lying about following Sam to her apartment. What the hell? I smelled you there."

"I've never been to her place in my life."

"Wolves don't lie. People do."

Owen's lips curled up over his teeth. "You want to poison her against me. She needs to understand we're meant to be together."

My head jerked back. "Excuse me?"

Marlon growled at his brother. Literally—*growled*. "Stay away from her."

"She was supposed to be mine," Owen declared.

"No, she wasn't!" snapped Marlon.

Pierre leapt to his feet, ready to break up a fight. Françoise tensed.

"I'm not a piece of meat!" I yelled. "And I'm not *meant* to be with anyone!"

"Sam," said Françoise gently, "the way it works with werewolves is you join your maker's pack."

"Maker?" I echoed.

But I already knew. Owen was the wolf who'd bitten me in Central Park. He'd risked killing me because he thought we were destined to be together? I remembered him saying: "I came to this concert to meet you." Why me?

Françoise looked across the table at her sons. She seemed to want them to tell me something, but they wouldn't meet my eyes. Too busy glaring at each other.

Suddenly, Owen grinned toothily, giving me a glimpse of his canines. Then he cocked his head, as if he were listening to something far away, slid out from behind the table, and plunged into the kitchen. A moment later, the outside door slammed shut.

Owen's parents stared stiffly at his empty chair. Marlon gulped down the last of his tea. Outside the dark window, I thought I saw the leaves rustle and a flash of brown streak past.

"Sam," murmured Françoise, "we're so sorry."

They were *sorry*? I didn't respond.

"How about I finish the story for you," suggested Marlon. "Okay, so my parents made it back to the States without getting caught. The farmer's death was blamed on a wild animal. All they wanted to do was hunt and eat. They dropped out of grad school, gathered some money, and started researching transmogrification: the change process."

"Wait. What do you mean by 'gathered' money?" I asked.

"Took it," said his mother bluntly. "Looted and robbed in wolf form, so no one could catch us. Believe me, those were horrible days. We're ashamed of how we acted. We had no control over any of our urges. Books and experts on the subject were hard to find. Well, good ones, anyway. There are so many rumors and legends. We didn't know anyone who could walk us through the changes."

"Dad still has a hard time controlling his urges," said Marlon. "So does Owen. We think it's because they were born with the wolf inside them, unlike the rest of us."

"How old were you?" I asked him.

He glanced at his parents. "Happened a week after they brought me home. An accident. They'd put me to bed and gone to sleep. When I woke up with a nightmare and snuck into their room, I guess I smelled like fresh meat to Dad. He snapped his jaws around my stomach and dragged me across the floor—"

"My own son," said Pierre, his voice cracking. "His tiny ribs snapped in my mouth. I still remember the sound."

"That night was awful," Françoise said softly. "I had to fight him off."

"I'll never forgive myself," said Pierre.

"Dad, I'm okay," said Marlon. "It was a long time ago."

Things could've been much worse these last few days. What if I'd attacked Jules, or Malika, or my mom? Or Harris? I couldn't think about any of that. I just needed to learn how to cope with the future. And Owen.

"Are we upsetting you? Should we stop?" asked Françoise.

I shook my head but couldn't form words.

"She needs to understand the danger," said Pierre. "She's been very lucky so far."

"Maybe she can control herself better than the rest of us for some reason," said Marlon. "Maybe there's something special about Sam. I mean, Mom survived the change, but there are so many horror stories about what happens to girls—death, mutations, insanity."

"What do you mean 'mutations'?" I asked.

"Some girls—the lucky ones, I guess—don't die. They just get stuck . . . can't fully change shape, and live in between. They're half a wolf. All the time."

Those two girls who'd jumped me yesterday—were they mutant werewolves? The fur and the claws were so realistic. I was reluctant to talk about the girls. Had Owen bitten them, too? Would his family stop him from doing it again, or cover up what he'd done?

"How many girls survive?" I asked.

The Lebruns glanced at one another.

"They mostly die," said Marlon.

"Like, how many of them?"

"Four out of five," admitted Françoise. "Or more. Honestly, we don't have enough case studies, but the ones we know about who survive all have mutations they can't conceal. One poor woman has the head of a wolf. She has to live as a recluse. Another just has a tail."

"I'm positive there's something special about you," Marlon said with a wink. But I could tell he was nervous.

"Maybe it's because I'm eating loads of meat," I said, eager to offer an explanation. "Which is a huge deal, considering I was a vegetarian for *years*."

Pierre frowned.

"Well, I have, uh, had a raging temper. And really vivid dreams about howling at the moon—"

"They probably weren't dreams," said Françoise.

"What?"

"Your body's been forcing you to change when you fall asleep," said Pierre. "To fulfill the wolf's urges."

Was he saying I may have done something horrible in the middle of the night? But I remembered my dog dreams, and they didn't involve murder. Although I'd almost made Zoe a midnight snack . . .

"What's going on during the day?" he asked.

"I keep wanting to do crazy stuff, like bite people and break things."

Pierre frowned again.

"Enough of this," said Françoise, clapping her hands. "Obviously, Sam's got much better self-control than any of us did."

Why did it sound like she was trying to convince me?

"We should be grateful for that," said Pierre, after a moment. "And now that she's found her pack, we'll help her."

I shook my head. "My pack?"

Pierre smiled and reached across the table to pat my hands, which were clenched together. "You're one of us. Every other werewolf you meet will smell Lebrun on you."

"Why?"

"It's in your blood," said Marlon.

"So I'm like your sister now? Your half-wolf sister?"

"Not exactly." The look he shot me was anything but brotherly.

"I think we should all go for a run," said Francoise, "and cool off. You need to experience the feeling of running with a pack, Sam. It's the most liberating thing in the world."

I would've loved to press PAUSE on my life and curl up with Janis or hang out with Malika, talking everything through until the sun came up. Mali always knew what to say. I'd probably never be able to tell her what was really going on with me again. It was all so messed up and unbelievable. I felt more alone than ever.

How could I trust these people? The Lebruns didn't seem particularly worried about trusting me with the knowledge that they were werewolves. But I'd learned that when you were somewhat famous like us, secrets could be worth a lot of money. I didn't need the cash. Clearly they didn't, either. Other people, though . . .

Pierre was staring out the window at the moon. I expected him to start howling any second. Were we going after Owen? My heart thumped, hard. They expected me to turn into a wolf. On demand?

In front of them? Would I have to watch them change, too? But I *was* curious. What did I look like when I was transforming?

Marlon's eyes were trained on the trees outside. His heart was already out there. He began to pick up the empty teacups. His mother put a hand on his arm.

"We'll clean up later."

Without looking at me, he headed for the kitchen. His parents followed. So did I.

The kitchen was designed in sterile black and chrome, an oddly stark and modern contrast to the antique decor in the rest of the house. We went out the back door onto a path that led straight into the woods. Manicured lawns and ornamental flower beds weren't a priority here. I squinted at the trees, wondering where Owen was.

Pierre lifted his shirt. He was going to change right now! Skin rippled, tightened, and stretched. His arms hunched up and shortened. When his pants began to fall away, I spun around. Once I heard him scamper into some nearby bushes, I decided it was safe to turn back. Instead of Pierre, a giant canine peered up at me. He looked just like the wolves who'd been in the park, except that his brown coat was shot through with gray.

"Please excuse my husband," said Françoise. "He's not used to guests."

"It's okay," I lied, feeling slightly queasy. "You're not expecting me to do that, are you?"

Marlon raised an amused eyebrow. "Shy?"

Françoise shook her head. "You don't need to be, Sam. Not around us."

"I think maybe I'll sit this one out. Stay at the house—"

"No way!" said Marlon. "You have to learn how to control the change, or it will control you. Sooner or later."

"And the only way to do that is to practice with us," said his mother. "Transforming here on our land with three experienced werewolves watching your back is a lot safer than prowling around the city alone."

She made a point.

"I'm not stripping in front of you," I told Marlon.

He laughed.

Françoise grabbed my hand and dragged me around the corner of the house, out of sight. Then she took off her clothes. Whoa. I'm not even that comfortable with my human body.

"The trick to changing—or not changing—is to control your mood and empty your mind," she said as she lowered to the ground on all fours. Her legs and hips melted into a wolf's haunches. "It's a little like meditation. Have you ever tried that?"

"My mom taught me a few relaxation techniques when my band first got really popular. I was having panic attacks every time I sat down to practice, and worse when I had to perform."

"Did it help?"

"Yeah. Some."

"Same sort of thing," said Françoise. As I watched, her hands became paws. They changed back to hands. Then paws again. Then hands. "Slow down your thoughts as much as possible and simply *will* your tissues and bones to give up their current shape. Or to remain as they are. After a while, it's no more difficult than forcing yourself to concentrate in any stressful situation. Try starting with a hand. . . ." One of her hands turned into a paw. "Close your eyes and imagine the change."

I took off my T-shirt and squeezed my eyes shut. I pictured Françoise's furry paws, then imagined my own hands changing shape and my nails lengthening into claws. Nothing happened. Not even a prickle beneath my skin. Sure enough, when I opened my eyes, I saw my same old black nail polish peeling off the tips of my fingernails. I sucked at this.

"You're trying too hard. It should feel natural. Clear your mind. Breathe. Gently nudge your body. It *wants* to transform."

I closed my eyes again and focused on the darkness and the earthy smells swirling around me: soil, trees, fragrant wildflowers, and beneath it all, Françoise's particular sweet wolfy odor. A tendril of thought reached out for my hands. The skin bubbled and stretched. Success! I kept my eyes shut so I wouldn't lose focus.

"Very good," whispered Françoise. "Now the rest of your body."

I finished my arms, then shifted my thoughts to my legs, pleading with them to become a wolf's hindquarters. They didn't respond. I got frustrated and had to take deep, slow breaths to relax again.

It didn't happen with the same grace as Françoise. It kind of happened all at once: my torso lengthened as my legs shook, and my skirt began to rip at the seams. I tore it off, pitched forward, and found myself spitting out dirt.

Paws aren't meant to balance a human's upper body. I felt like puking. Then it passed. My sports bra stretched to its limits and cut into flesh—then snapped right off. The bulk of my stomach moved upward, into my chest. I rolled onto my back and scrambled to claw off any remaining scraps of clothing. I finished by transforming my head.

Françoise stood above me in wolf form, panting her approval. As a wolf, she was also small and round.

My wolf appendages worked more like closed fists than hands and feet. But my limbs felt . . . free. I stretched forward, then back. Stuck out my tongue as far as it would go. A gust of wind ruffled my fur. Wow. This shape felt fantastic. *Normal.*

Françoise nudged my shoulder with her snout in greeting. I gnashed my teeth, not sure I wanted her getting so close to my throat. She still smelled okay, though. Like old books and tea. Also— to my surprise—like family.

CHAPTER 11

WHEN FRANÇOISE SURGED forward into the forest, I followed awkwardly, adjusting to my new perspective on the world. These legs moved strangely. Sometimes one at a time, sometimes two on opposite sides. I became highly conscious of my movements and lumbered along, until I figured out a rhythm where my balance switched from side to side.

My vision was a confusing series of close-ups. It was much easier to piece together information about my surroundings by using my nose and ears. But since my nose was low to the ground, smells could be distracting. At least I didn't have to look around to locate Françoise. I just had to lift my snout. The wind swept her scent in my direction.

She remained ahead of me but would pause to look back every few steps. Her jaw hung open, as if she was trying to smile, and her tongue lolled to one side. Her fur was exactly the same color as her human hair—reddish brown with a white streak on the top. When she veered off to the left, through pungent evergreens, I staggered behind, feeling like a toddler learning to walk. If I didn't pay attention, my snout would drag along the ground. After a couple nosefuls of grass, I learned to hold it up.

Through the trees I caught a glimpse of Pierre—slimmer and

longer than his wife. He turned to yip hello and bounded over to me. Marlon loped up behind him, sleek and dark brown. I stiffened and backed away, trembling. There was no doubt he was one of the wolves who'd jumped me in Central Park! When he came running up to sniff me, I gnashed my teeth in his direction.

There was a loud crash in the woods. I twisted around and saw Owen racing up to us at full speed. He was nearly identical to his brother, just a little wider around the torso and shoulders. I smelled him cautiously, then backed away. His scent was powerful and familiar. I was so distracted that I backed up into a prickly bush and yelped.

Pierre barked once, sharply, then raced off. The pack swept after him. I joined them before I even realized I was moving, though I was so clumsy, I quickly fell behind. The sight of them running together was amazing: fur rippling in the wind, muscles bunching and releasing with each leap. They owned this forest.

An iridescent beetle's carapace glinted as it scuttled across a flat rock. I catapulted through the air to land on top of it, in the process disrupting a mama raccoon who was weaving through the brush with her young. She screeched and clawed the air near my nose. I growled and reared on my haunches. She nudged her tasty-looking babies away from me with her hind legs but held her ground. The little ones skittered into a hollow log to hide. I barked fiercely and feinted at the mom. She ran into the log. I lowered myself to peer inside and could see their four sets of eyes gleaming, but my paws couldn't reach that far.

The Lebruns discovered I'd stopped following and came running to see what was going on. Marlon inserted himself protectively between me and the mother raccoon. The other wolves flanked us. I lunged at the log, which was useless. Then out of the corner of my eye, I noticed my tail wagging. I gave up on the raccoons and chased my tail around in circles until I got dizzy and staggered to a stop. It took me a moment to recover. So much fun! A built-in party game.

The Lebruns just stood there watching. Then Pierre barked at me and bounded farther into the woods. His family ran along behind him, calling to me with little barks. They soon disappeared. I started to panic, but Marlon reappeared; and as I followed, he slowed down to stay nearby. From time to time he moved close enough to prod me with his snout.

Marlon had endless patience as he waited for me to explore the crags and crannies of the forest. I stumbled a million times but didn't hurt myself. It was much easier to get back up now that I had four feet. And there was a lot less distance to fall. Losing my footing was kind of fun, too, like doing a somersault.

Once in a while Owen would jump up on a high rock or log and howl. Marlon and I had to join in—the sound was infectious. Howling was as cathartic as playing music. And just like my band, the other pack wolves responded to the sound. Sometimes we were together and other times far apart. We used howls to keep track of one another.

I paused to smell everything. Each mushroom was different, but all were musky and earthy. An anthill was a bland stew, and a hole in the ground smelled strongly of wet rabbit. As I turned away from it, a nearby bush shook. Its inhabitant was hoping I wouldn't notice. I snuffled excitedly, and the terrified creature started hopping, revealing itself to Marlon as well.

He moved forward in a stealth crouch. I tried to mimic his movements. He leapt. I did, too. We sailed through the air toward the bush, smashed heads, and fell to the ground, whining in pain. The plump rabbit took the opportunity to hop off safely. I lay there, seeing stars.

Marlon recovered first, staggered to his feet, and growled at me to leave the hunting to him. Then he trotted away in a huff and led us to the rest of the pack, who were closer than I'd thought. Pierre waited attentively on a big rock in a clearing. When we approached, he snapped his jaw at us, which I interpreted to mean "stay quiet."

Marlon lowered his body and crept forward to where his mother lay half hidden behind a tree trunk. She was almost entirely camouflaged by the thick ground covering. I couldn't see Owen, but I smelled him close by. My heart raced. I crawled after Marlon. I'd made it only a few feet when one of my front paws snapped a twig. Whoops. Marlon's head whipped around. Françoise's jaws vibrated in a silent growl.

What was going on? She sounded wary. I continued to pick my way through the foliage, choosing carefully where to place each paw so I wouldn't make any noise. Up ahead, there was a bush big enough to hide me. I maneuvered myself so that I was mostly underneath it. A whiff of something delicious reached me: a gamey scent I couldn't place.

I scrambled forward a couple more steps until my nose was lined up with Françoise's, as if we were waiting at a starting line. Finally, I could see what all the excitement was about. Directly in front of us was a young deer, stooping to drink from a stream. The wolves were poised to bring it down. I tried to prepare myself mentally, but I felt like a fake—I wanted to run in the other direction. I couldn't attack Bambi. Some all-powerful beast I was!

Owen appeared on the far side of the deer. His father crept out of the shadows beside him. How had they gotten all the way to the other side of the clearing without making a sound? The poor creature was oblivious.

Françoise growled loudly enough for the deer to hear her. It lifted its head, ears and nostrils twitching. Françoise feinted forward. The deer bolted, right into the path of Owen and Pierre, who lunged toward it, making it backtrack in our direction.

The deer was light and quick. It would have gained ground and escaped, but then Marlon leapt up, startling it just long enough for Owen to snap his teeth around its short tail. The animal thrashed and kicked. It caught Owen squarely in the shoulder, and he fell back. The deer was running again. Marlon jumped back and forth, as if he was playing with it. Pierre rushed forward from behind and raked his claw down a hind leg.

That meat smelled so good. Blood filled my brain.

I charged, wanting to help my pack. I knew the Lebruns had deliberately set this up. They were letting me finish off the fawn—it would be my first conscious kill. And I was going to do it.

Then the deer made eye contact with me. I could see its terror. Suddenly, I remembered exactly how I felt when I was jumped by two ferocious wolves alone in the park. I skidded to a halt.

The deer took advantage of my confusion to butt me with its stubby antlers, which sent me flying into Marlon. The stunned animal stood there for a moment. I barked at it to run away, and it tried, but its injured leg wasn't working properly. Yowling in frustration, Owen circled around and clamped his jaws onto its neck. The deer went down without a fight. Owen snapped his head from side to side, cracking bones, then dragged the carcass back to my feet, offering me the fresh kill. The deer's unmoving eyes stared up at me.

I inched away. Owen yipped, jumped forward, and ripped out

the deer's throat for me. Warm blood spread across the undergrowth. Pierre dived and began to lap it up. Françoise put one paw on a deer leg and tore off some flesh. She backed up to make room for her two sons.

If there was any part of me that still doubted I was a real werewolf, watching them eat convinced me. Every fiber of my being urged me to join the feast. But I felt dizzy from the blow to the head, and I stumbled into the forest.

Once I was away from the smell, my skin began to prickle, and my human side tried to surface. Damn! I had no clothes! My panic forced the rest of the change. I jumped behind a tree, just in time to avoid giving Marlon a free show. He barked questioningly.

"Turn around!" I yelled at him, unsure if he understood what I was saying. He must have, because he swung his head back. I began to make my way through the woods toward the house, trying to stay out of sight. The sky was lightening, so even my human eyes could see several feet in front of me.

After waiting a few seconds, Marlon barreled after me. I couldn't let him see me like this! I started to run and tripped over a fallen branch. He easily caught up but passed right by without looking and loped along slightly ahead.

When we reached the house, Marlon jumped onto the back steps while I lingered behind a bush. He howled to inform the other wolves we were home. Then he quickly changed shape and bent over to pull on his jeans, causing me to blush from my hiding spot. He picked up the rest of his clothes and opened the door.

"You can get dressed now, Sam."

I hurried around to the side of the house where I'd left my clothes. Before I could finish dressing, Marlon peeked around the corner.

"Can't you give me a little privacy?" I yanked down my shirt and walked over to the door.

"What's going on?" he asked.

"That animal! Its terror . . . all the blood. It brought back that night when you and Owen attacked me. How *could* you?"

He winced. "Yeah, I figured— I'm sorry, Sam. I couldn't stop my brother."

Owen hurtled out of the bushes, transforming in midstride. I glanced down at my feet as soon as I saw the edge of his body shudder, but I was too late. I saw it all. Thankfully, Pierre and Françoise grabbed their clothes between their teeth, peered at me in a disturbingly intelligent way, and discreetly headed around the corner.

When Françoise returned, she looked at me with concern. "Is everything all right?"

"Sam's fine," said Marlon. "She just got spooked."

"*Spooked?* The other day, your brother almost murdered *me* like that deer."

Marlon looked at the ground guiltily.

Owen didn't. He rolled his eyes. "Oh, please."

"The hunt was too much," said their mother sympathetically. "We were trying to help you adjust."

"Too much, too fast!" I told her. "Definitely."

Owen's gaze moved rapidly from his mother to me. He made a face that said he was fed up with all of us. "We thought you'd been injured. You almost made us lose our prey."

I crossed my arms and glared at him.

He turned and stalked back into the woods, calling over his shoulder, "I'm still hungry!"

The other three Lebruns stared longingly in Owen's direction for a few moments, then entered the kitchen.

As soon as I stepped inside, I felt how tired I was. Exhausted. I mumbled something about needing a ride home and dragged myself toward the front door. When I passed the living room, I noticed that their sofa looked incredibly comfortable. My intention was only to sit down for a minute before getting Marlon to drive me back into the city, but he didn't follow me into the room fast enough.

There were a few books lying on the coffee table. I flipped them over. The one that looked the most interesting was by an animal psychologist who'd studied the characteristics shared by particularly violent species. Rather than blaming the animals for their natural urges, he advocated for nature preserves where humans weren't allowed. The author was Armando Rojas. Rojas—that name again, like the guy in Words of Wonder. . . . But I was too tired to read. I put down the book, laid my head on the armrest, and was immediately asleep.

At some point Marlon showed up carrying a plate with four meat sandwiches and a jug of water. When I awoke fully, the plate was on the coffee table, and he'd pushed my legs aside so he could sit next to me. It wasn't a big couch, more like a love seat. His arm was up against mine, and whenever he moved, it was distracting. He seemed to be moving quite a bit, picking up sandwiches, holding them up to my mouth until I took bites, pouring glass after glass of water, lifting those for me, too. I didn't have the energy to fight.

"It takes a lot out of you—the change," he said. "Plus, your body's probably still adjusting to the demands of your inner wolf. Eating will help."

I opened my mouth to refuse, but he stuffed a sandwich in it.

I tried to bat his hand away but was too weak. The meat was really raw. Wait. Was it deer?! Before I could demand to know what I was inhaling, Marlon shoved another glass of water to my mouth. I gulped it down.

"Want more?" he asked between mouthfuls of his own sandwich.

"What's this?" I mumbled.

"Beef."

He was lying. I considered protesting, but he gave me the last sandwich, along with a fresh glass of water, and I ended up munching instead. So good. And I did feel stronger. I lowered my head to the armrest again.

Sometime later, I awoke with a jolt when my cell phone beeped in my pocket. It was a text from Vinnie, saying he'd booked me a slot on *The Wanda Show* for tomorrow. She'd had a last-minute cancellation and the leaked photo made me big news. I groaned and responded with two letters: OK.

Marlon was lounging beside me with his eyes closed, one hand resting on my thigh. I shoved it away and jabbed him in the ribs with my elbow. Morning light came through the window. Passing out in a house filled with werewolves wasn't the safest move I'd ever made.

"I need you to drive me home," I said.

Marlon opened his eyes a crack and yawned. "My parents made up the guest room for you. I'll drive you back to the city this afternoon, when I go to meet with a prof."

"Thanks, but I want my own bed." Except that my Brooklyn apartment seemed so far away, and I was *still* tired. Marlon didn't look like he was in any shape to be driving, either. "All right. Where's the room? And does the door lock?"

He waved a hand toward the kitchen. "It locks. I can carry you, if you want."

"Maybe in an alternate universe. But in this one, I've got a shred of dignity left."

He grinned saucily. "I wouldn't mind meeting Alternate Universe Sam someday."

I stood up quickly and almost toppled over. Going back to sleep as soon as possible was the *only* safe thing I could do at that moment. There was so much to learn about being a werewolf, like how long I needed to recharge my internal batteries. The side of the sofa kept me upright until the world stopped spinning. Then I took a couple of steps and passed out.

This time when I opened my eyes, Marlon was putting me on a king-size bed. Apparently, I was the fainting-daisy kind of werewolf. So much for dignity.

My cell phone beeped again: a text from Jules. She was pissed about the photo and accused me of hogging the spotlight with the Wanda interview. An important band meeting was now scheduled at Mali's for this afternoon. I'd better not miss it, or Jules would make sure I got voted off the island.

The guest room was extravagantly decorated, with plush carpeting, matching furniture, and every convenience, including a mini fridge. A home entertainment system took up one whole wall, and picture windows made up another one. The view was of the spot where Françoise had taken me to change. I slumped into the pillows and shivered as I peered out at the tree trunks and bushes. Maybe somewhere out there Owen was eating the remains of the deer, all by himself. I could almost hear the sound of tearing flesh.

Marlon walked around the bed, blocking my line of sight. "Bathroom's through there." He pointed. "I recommend the hot tub."

"Just don't sneak in and take any pictures," I said. He frowned. "Sorry. Never mind."

"Well, the bathroom locks, too. We almost never have people stay over now that Grandma's passed away, so it kind of goes to waste."

That got my attention. "This was your dead grandmother's room?"

"She didn't *die* in here, Sam. We didn't even see her much as I got older."

"Did your grandma know what you are?"

"She may have suspected because of the legends," he said. "But my parents were afraid to tell her. I like to think she would have accepted me."

I only nodded. How would my mother react? Could I ever tell her what had happened to me?

Of course my assumption his grandmother had died here was stupid, but I was thrown off by him standing there at the foot of the bed, staring at me, all concerned for my well-being. He'd just carried me into bed! And he seemed to be saving me a lot lately. It crossed my mind that he might be hoping for an invitation to join me under the sheets. Two guys in less than 24 hours.

"I'm going to sleep now," I said.

Marlon didn't move. "That's a really big bed."

"Out!"

He smothered another grin and crossed to the door. "Don't worry, I'm locking this for you. You're safe and sound."

I held my breath until I heard the click of the lock.

CHAPTER 12

ONCE I WAS ALONE IN THE ROOM, I went over to the windows and shut the blackout blinds, then I went into the bathroom. My reflection in the mirror looked wild and haggard. My clothes were a disaster, there were smudges of dirt on my cheek, and my hair was poking out in all directions. I tugged open the cabinet and discovered a stack of toothbrushes still in their packagings. A soak in the Jacuzzi would feel incredible, but I didn't want to risk passing out in there. I washed my face and hands, wrapped myself in a fluffy white robe I found hanging on the back of the door, and brushed my teeth. Then I climbed into the ridiculously huge bed. The room was pitch-black from the blinds. As I lay there, I couldn't help picturing all the creepy crawly things lurking outside those windows. I missed the sounds and streets of the city.

The next time I opened my eyes, there was a horrible tightness in my chest. My arms wouldn't—no, couldn't—move. Something heavy was pinning me down. *Someone.* Sitting on my chest. He growled. I recognized his smell. Owen!

I tried to scream, but there was no oxygen in my lungs. Owen growled again, leaned down, and shoved his hairy snout into my face. His pointed teeth pressed against my cheek. Warm saliva leaked

onto my chin. I struggled, knowing it was useless. He was much too strong.

"Samantha," he whispered, his voice still strangely human.

"Uhhnn," I wheezed pitifully, when what I wanted was to scream "Get the hell off me!"

His weight lifted for an instant. I sucked in a lungful of air and let out a shriek. He pressed his hairy face against my mouth to shut me up. I chomped down as hard as I could, then twisted and tried to roll, freeing my shoulders but causing his claws to sink into my chest and upper arms, piercing fabric and skin.

Pain and adrenaline gave me another rush, and suddenly I was transforming. My skin prickled and bubbled; my body mass shifted. The change made it impossible for him to keep me pinned. I rolled and scrambled out from beneath him, trembling and snarling. He swung around to face me. I gnashed at his neck and actually hit my target. My teeth sliced through the tangle of fur and sank into flesh. He whimpered and tried to shake me off, but not hard enough to force me to tear out his jugular. His back legs lost their grip, and he fell off the bed. I released my hold, unwilling to go in for the kill.

Owen stood. Although he was bleeding pretty badly, he didn't seem scared. I braced myself for another attack. His head cocked to one side. He'd heard something. Then I heard it, too: a series of hollow slaps. Feet hitting wooden stairs.

"Sam?" yelled Françoise, banging on the door.

Owen spun toward the picture windows. He jumped. The blinds crumpled as he smashed into them and kept going right through the glass, which exploded into fragments. Sunlight burned my eyes. I squeezed them shut and held up my arms. Shards of glass embedded in my skin. I ran to the empty window frame, ignoring the glass, and shaded my eyes as I watched Owen race away into the woods.

Before I could catch my breath, someone slammed open the door. Claws drawn, I hurled toward the new threat—Marlon—and bowled him over. We tumbled onto the carpet. He remained in human form, groggy and shocked. But I couldn't stop. My teeth pressed against his throat.

His mother entered the room and screamed, "Stop, Sam!"

I growled.

"What are you doing?" asked Marlon from underneath me.

Wanting to hurt them both—make them feel what I felt—I dug my claws into Marlon's shoulder. In a blur he transformed, and his pajama bottoms tore away. He allowed me to keep him pinned, but his vibrating growl told me that I wouldn't get off the hook so easily if I hurt him a second time.

Marlon hadn't attacked me, I reminded myself, taking a shaky breath that ended in a hiccup-y bark. But he *had* told me to feel safe in this room. I jumped off him, padded into the bathroom, and made myself human again. It took a long time because I was so upset and couldn't focus. When the change was finally complete, I pulled out a few stinging glass shards from my arms and washed the scrapes, wrapped the big robe around myself, and went back out to the bedroom. Pierre had joined them.

"Locked door, huh?" I said. "Was this all part of your plan? Trapping me in your house!"

"What are you talking about?" asked Françoise. She seemed so vulnerable, standing there in her cotton nightgown. A nervous tick flicked in her right eye.

Marlon, back in human form, had grabbed the comforter off the bed and wrapped it around his waist. His spiky hair flopped to one side, and he looked confused, like a little boy woken up too early.

"Calm down, Sam," he said. "We don't know what's going on."

"Don't you dare tell me to calm d-down!" I yelled—damn hiccups. "Y-you convinced me that your family was all right and f-fed me sandwiches. This is all a g-game to you, isn't it?"

"I was sound asleep when you smashed that window!"

"I d-didn't!"

Pierre looked increasingly alarmed. "What the hell is going on?"

I held my breath for a moment to calm down. It got rid of the hiccups. "As if you don't know. Owen attacked me!"

"But he's upstairs in bed," said Françoise.

"No, he's not! Unless werewolves have the power to be in two places at once. Or to climb walls." As soon as I said the second part, I pictured the cracked paint on my fourth-floor window. *Shit.*

"Did you have a nightmare?" Pierre asked. "I don't remember exactly what it was like for me in those early days, but—"

"I woke up with Owen on top of me. If I hadn't gotten loose, I'd probably be dead. Go check his room!"

Françoise rushed out. Pierre and Marlon stayed behind, obviously trying to figure out what to say. I snatched up my clothes and ran back to the bathroom—the last thing I wanted to hear was stupid excuses or rationalizations.

Tears filled my eyes. I couldn't believe I was crying. The Lebruns didn't deserve it. But I'd started to like them—well, Marlon and his parents. Locking the little latch, which was too flimsy to do any good, I put on my clothes, then sank down onto the floor with my back against the door. The only window in the room was too high to climb out. Or in. I was grateful to feel the weight of my cell phone and keys in my hoodie pocket.

There was a gentle *tap-tap-tap*ping on the door.

"Sam?" said Françoise as she rattled the knob.

"Back off!"

"Please come out and talk to us."

"No way. Owen bit me in the park, and I nearly bled to death. Now he's hoping to finish me off."

The rattling stopped.

"Sam," said Marlon, "it's more complicated than—"

"Just shut up!" I snarled. "Stop making excuses."

"We're not," said Françoise. "I promise. You were right. Owen isn't in his room."

I exhaled sharply. "I can't believe the whole world thinks you guys are awesome. What a joke."

"My son is . . . troubled," she said. "I've known this for a while, but now I have to face it."

"Please, just leave me alone. I want to go home."

"We're all so sorry," she said.

I pulled out my cell, dialed my mom's number, and listened to it ring. Damn it, no answer. She was off to Toronto. What was I going to say, anyway? I hung up and pretended to leave a message, speaking loudly enough for them to hear. "Hey, it's Sam. I'm in Pierre and Françoise Lebrun's home—you know, the famous professors from NYU—and I'm in serious trouble—"

Someone was pounding on the door.

"—I'm scared. They're a pack of werewolves. Seriously, werewolves! I'm one, too—the good kind, not the kind that eats people. It's hard to believe, I know. Their son attacked me. Now I'm locked in the bathroom." I began to laugh hysterically, muffling the sound in a bath towel. If this voice mail were real, it would be the strangest ever.

"Sam, get off the phone!" yelled Pierre.

"If I don't make it home by the time you get this message, call the police and send them to Long Island. I don't have the exact address, but I doubt there are many Lebruns out here, and it's a huge property. I love you. Bye!"

"Who did you just call?" demanded Marlon.

"My mother. Now she knows where I am. She'll call the cops if you don't let me go."

"We can't get the police involved," said Francoise.

"I hope they haul you all off to the pound," I said, putting the phone in my pocket.

"Think about what you're doing," she pleaded. "If the police find out about us, they also find out about you. They'll do a lot more than lock us up."

"Just leave Marlon's keys on the bed and let me walk out of the house with them."

I heard a groan from Marlon. "Not my car again. This is crazy. We would never attack you."

"One of you already did. Twice. If you let me go *right now*, I'll erase that message before my mother hears it. If not, then cops will be swarming around here in an hour. . . ."

"If you don't erase it," said Françoise, "it would be very bad—for our pack."

My pack. I was now a member of the werewolf demographic. Permanently. Overnight, I'd gone from being a girl whose worst secret was cheating on her veggie diet to having something I needed to keep buried—because my life depended on it. Images of a top secret government unit that operated outside the law sprang to mind. I could end up being poked and prodded, living out the rest of my life in a cage, like one of those poor test monkeys. And if the cops investigated, so would the media. I didn't know which was worse. I shook my head to clear the picture of my hairy face on the cover of *Us Weekly*.

"We're trying to help you," said Marlon.

"Leave me your keys! The sooner you do, the sooner I can—"

"Okay."

I listened to Marlon run out of the room, come back, and shake the keys. "They're on the bed," he said. "We're going outside."

Once I heard the bedroom door shut, I came out and cautiously peeked around. No one was there. Aside from the wind whooshing through the broken window, I heard nothing.

I grabbed the keys and walked down the hall. The kitchen door was slightly ajar. Owen had indeed gone back for the deer: its skinned carcass, minus a haunch, hung from a hook in the ceiling. Ugh. So that explained all the steel. But the smell tempted rather than repulsed me. I hurried out the front door toward the El Camino.

I didn't see the Lebruns anywhere. I slid into the driver's seat and took off down the road. Then I noticed a glint in my rearview mirror. Someone was behind me, on a motorcycle. Marlon? He followed me onto the highway—but he wasn't trying to catch up. That I was driving his car home from Long Island for the second time *was* a little ridiculous.

The snarl of New York traffic gave me a chance to think. Maybe Owen really had acted alone. The rest of his family seemed so shocked. But what about the fact that he'd bitten me in the first place? I was glad I'd gotten out of there. I'd survived. I was a survivor. A weregirl, but one who could still use her human wits.

Pulling up near my building, I tossed the keys onto the front seat and left the car unlocked, knowing Marlon was probably waiting just around the corner. I triple-checked the security system on my way in, not that doors seemed to stop these wolf boys. Upstairs, the first thing I did was change my clothes, then I headed into the kitchen to drink a gallon of water. The window above the stove was wide-open again. Huh? I glanced at the table and nearly had another breakdown. Deep claw marks scarred its surface, spelling out a message: *I SAID STAY AWAY FROM OWEN.*

Without waiting to learn if the message writer was still around, I backed out of the kitchen, grabbed Janis, and left the apartment. My body ached. I needed somewhere to rest and heal. It felt like time was slipping away from me. Our band meeting was only a few hours off, and we had our show tonight at the Cake Shop; I had to get myself under control fast.

In the stairwell, I called Malika. She answered on the third ring. "Mmph'lo?"

"Mali. It's me, Sam. Sorry to wake you, but I—"

"Huh?" There was a rustle of sheets.

"I need somewhere to crash until the meeting."

"Whazzat?"

"I'm coming over now. Can I hang out on your couch?"

More noise in the background. When she spoke again, her voice sounded clearer. "Sure. What's wrong with your place?"

"I . . . uh . . . I've got a stalker. Or two."

And so began the endless lies to cover up my hairy truth.

"Nobody can get into your building with that new system you installed."

"Yeah, well, they've already done that. More than once."

"Who?"

"Marlon. And his brother. I don't want to see them ever again."

"What is it? Drugs? Do you owe them money? I thought you were all straightedge . . . but you've been really off lately. If you tell me what's going on, I can help."

"It's not drugs, Mali. I swear. I just need a place to chill for a couple hours."

"You should call the cops—they've helped us in the past with stalker fans."

"I have," I said, burying myself further in lies. "These guys are slippery. Look, I barely slept last night. I need to pass out."

She paused a second. "Of course. You can take my bed. I'm wide awake now."

"Thanks. I'm on my way."

Now I just needed to make sure nobody followed me. I called a car service and stepped out of my building warily, scanning every angle. It seemed like a regular day on the street. A guy was smoking in front of the cigar shop—he noticed me staring and blew smoke in my direction.

Turning away, I found myself face-to-face with Ponytail Girl. She wore a baggy sweatshirt with the hood pulled down low to cover up the fur.

"Dammit, where'd you come from?"

She didn't answer, just seized my shoulders with hands covered in mismatched mittens and shook me hard. I was so worn-out that I didn't even fight back.

"Where is she? Tell me!" she yelled.

"Who? Let me go!"

"Hey!" shouted the guy across the street.

"My friend Sue. Where is she?"

"How should I know?"

The guy was suddenly pulling her off me. "Break it up!"

I really didn't need a Good Samaritan right now. Had the guy called the police? He didn't seem like the type who'd do that. And there hadn't been enough time? The girl turned away abruptly, hiding her face in the hood.

He shook his head and glanced at me. "Are you okay?"

"Yeah," I said. "I think we're fine over here. Thanks, though."

He crossed back to the store, muttering about having only a five-minute break and wasting it on refereeing a cat fight.

More like a dog fight, but close enough.

The wolf girl couldn't have been more than sixteen. Despite my irritation, I felt sorry for her.

"What's going on?" I asked, touching her arm.

She jerked away. "I haven't seen her since early this morning, when she ran off to your place. Tell me what you did to her."

"Me? She's the one who left that threat."

"Threat?" The girl shrugged.

"She owes me a new table."

"I don't care about that! Where is she?"

My car rounded the corner. I waved at the driver. "It hasn't been that long. She'll show up."

"No, something's wrong. We stay together during the day. It's safer. Sue and I are like family. I'm all she's got now."

The driver pulled up to the curb. The girl yanked the strings on her hood tighter.

"I'm *so* screwed," she whimpered. "Sue's taken off. I'm hideous. I have no one."

"What's your name?" I asked, reluctant to let her go.

"Queenie," she said as she turned away from me.

"What do you know about Owen Lebrun?" I asked her.

I signaled the driver to wait and looked back at her. But she was gone.

CHAPTER 13

MALIKA'S SHOE BOX ONE-BEDROOM near Central Park had cost her almost as much as my dilapidated pickle factory in Brooklyn. Her uniformed doorman always made me feel totally awkward by ushering me in with a hammy grin and a flourish of his cap. But he'd help keep out unwanted visitors, so I wasn't about to complain.

The elevator up to the fifteenth floor was a smooth ride, unlike my own rusty clunker. Malika poked her head out of her apartment as the doors opened. The doorman had called up to announce my arrival.

"It sucks that you're afraid to be alone in your apartment," she said.

"Yeah," I replied at my most eloquent.

"Why do these guys feel entitled to invade your private sanctuary?"

"I have no idea."

"Curse all the guys out there who make us feel unsafe!"

"Ha, yeah. The girls, too. Maybe *after* I take that nap," I said, trying to lighten the mood.

She smiled, stepped forward with arms raised, and waited for me to stumble into the hug. Her warmth and scent enveloped me: jasmine oil and soap and coffee. While I was being hugged by Malika, everything felt okay.

She pulled back and waited, expecting me to start talking. I wished I could tell her everything, but I just sighed and bit my lip. When she realized I wasn't going to confide in her, she welcomed me into the apartment without a word—another reason I loved her.

"I'm dead tired," I said.

"Scoot, scoot—go sleep." She waved me toward her bedroom. "I'm making pancakes and tofu bacon for brunch. It'll be on the table when you wake up."

"You rock," I said, shutting the bedroom door. I stripped down to tank top and tights, and slid beneath the cool sheets. Nothing bad could happen to me here. Giving in to exhaustion felt right. My dreams didn't even turn into nightmares.

Malika woke me by popping her head into the room. "Jules and Vinnie are on their way over."

"Huh?" I shot upright, and the change bubbled beneath my skin. My cheeks prickled. Hair was sprouting in front of Malika! I clapped a pillow to my face. My claws pierced the linen. I flopped back down and whipped the comforter over my head.

"Are you okay?" she asked, coming closer.

"Just need a moment."

I lay still, breathing loudly, trying to convince my body that my best friend was standing there—not my enemy. There was no reason to get hairy. But my body wouldn't believe me. I tried meditating: "Ommmmmmmmmm."

"Are you humming under there?" asked Malika, standing right next to me.

"You scared me!" I yelped, pulling the comforter tighter.

"You're hiding?"

"Maybe."

"You're acting so weird these days. I hate that stalker guys have gotten under your skin."

Under my skin was right. "Don't worry about me. I'll be good once I eat some of your incredible pancakes. Just . . . let me wake up on my own, okay?"

"Okay . . . Well, heat 'em up in the micro first, because you've been asleep for hours. They're stone-cold. But the pot of coffee in the kitchen is fresh."

When she was gone, I swung my legs over the side of the bed. They looked normal. My hands still had claws, but they returned to fingertips after a few deep breaths. Thank god. I was eager to get caffeine into my system. I walked out of the bedroom, sniffing the air.

"You're the best friend a girl could have!" I called out to her.

Malika yelled back from the living room: "If genius songwriter Sam Lee says so, then it must be true!"

The beat of her drums drifted into the bathroom while I washed my face and worked a little gel into my hair. She was practicing "Cry Little Soldiers" as quietly as possible. Her apartment was soundproof, like mine, so we could play here occasionally without the neighbors getting pissed.

In the kitchen, I picked out the biggest mug in the cabinet—it qualified as a bucket. There were dancing cows on the side with the message: "Sometimes you just have to wake up and smell the shit." I began to caffeinate. The stack of pancakes and tofu bacon would've been much better fresh, but they were still edible. She'd made the tofu for my sake. Maybe she thought the sandwiches at the video shoot were a slip? And the chicken photo?

Pouring a second cup of coffee drained her pot, so I started another one, then picked at my bass while she played the drums until the doorman called up to announce Jules's arrival. My sense of calm evaporated. Jules could always get to me.

Today she looked like a willowy wood nymph in green tights, a brown dress, and half a dozen scarves. Her hair was streaked with emerald dye, which drew attention to her dark eyes. Their stormy gaze told me everything I needed to know about her state of mind. I wished I'd called her back. She opened her portable keyboard and pressed a key. B-flat rang out like a warning.

"Got over your hissy fit yet?" asked Jules.

"Hello to you, too," I said. "I've been going through . . . something rough. I've been sick. Food poisoning."

"Sam's also got some really determined stalkers," chipped in Malika, earning herself a glare from Jules. "That friend of Harris's who hung out backstage for a while after the last show and his brother. They've been breaking into her place."

"He seemed normal enough to me," said Jules, sitting down on the couch.

"He's not," I snapped.

"Whatevs. Let's get this meeting started. Where's Vinnie?"

"You can't even get off your throne long enough to be worried about me, can you?" I demanded.

"Don't make this about me. *You're* the issue," said Jules, running a finger up and down the keys. "We gotta walk on eggshells because of you. You're the only reason our band exists. You're the talented one. You're the one Wanda Kalamata worships. You, you, you. You can even act like a total witch and ruin our video shoot and not call anyone for forty-eight hours, because no one else has the balls to tell you off. How do you expect us to react?"

Is that what they really thought of me? Stricken, I glanced at Malika.

"Leave me out of this," said Malika, shaking her head. Her phone rang with the doorman's special tone, and she went into the kitchen to answer it.

"At least now I know you don't give two shits about me," I said to Jules. "Just how things affect you."

She rolled her eyes and crossed her arms. The three of us waited in silence until Vinnie came in, wearing his favorite purple tracksuit. He had more hair on his stubbly chin than his head, which he kept shaved down to a quarter-inch to disguise the fact that it was thinning.

"How're my ladies?" he asked, holding out his arms for a group hug. He didn't let anyone opt out. I cringed the whole time. My inner wolf had turned my boundaries into barbed wire fences.

"Malika, it's your turn to chair," said Jules, ending the hug. "So get on with it."

"Don't talk to her like that," I said. "You're not her boss."

Vinnie's eyebrows rose. He wasn't used to having *two* divas in the room.

"I wrote down a list of issues that have come up recently," said Malika. She pulled a sheet of paper from under Jules's keyboard case. "First, we need to reschedule the video shoot."

"Pronto. The post-production studio has back-to-back projects lined up," said Vinnie. "If they don't get the raw footage soon, we'll have to find someone else to cut the damn thing."

"That's really a Sam problem," said Jules.

"Sam seems fine," said Vinnie. "Can we resched for Thursday?"

That was only four days from now. I took a gulp of coffee to stop myself from protesting. I was a big girl. I'd have to get over my issues with heat and lights, because they were part of my life. I could practice at the gig tonight.

"Sure," I said, clenching my mug and burying my face in it.

Malika jotted down "Thursday" next to that agenda item. "We've had a bunch of requests to play festivals next summer, and Vinnie's been booking us all over the place." She passed around printouts with calendars on them. Mali was always the organized one. "There's a conflict, see? Phoenix and Miami are on the same weekend. Anyone have a preference?"

"Sam?" said Jules. "You're the one who dictates everything."

"Shut up," I spat, then shocked myself by whipping my mug at her.

She ducked in time. It smashed against the wall, and coffee dripped down in a puddle onto the floor. For a moment we all sat there gaping at the broken ceramic. I couldn't believe I'd just done that!

Someone's cell phone rang. Oh, mine. I rummaged in the bottom of my bag. No one ever called me other than the people who were in that room. And my mom.

It was my home number on the display screen.

"Who's this?"

"Me," said Marlon. "I'm waiting for you to get home."

"How'd you get in?"

"Window. We need to talk. About the message carved into your table. Also, your boyfriend called a minute ago. I was forced to listen to him gush all over your voice mail about how sorry he was for drinking too much."

I moved into the kitchen, away from the others. "Harris isn't my boyfr— Uhn! How'd you get my password? You make me crazy. Do you know some girl named Sue?"

"Everyone knows someone named Sue. Why?"

"She was with your brother at The Puffs concert. She and her furry friend, Queenie, jumped me and told me to stay away from him. Then Queenie accosted me this morning, demanding to know what happened to Sue."

"What happened to Sue?"

"I don't know. But I think both girls are mutant wolves. Have you seen Owen?"

"No. Come over here now. You're not safe."

"And I'll be safe with you? Leave my apartment or I'll find your precious car and do some damage."

"Don't be stupid."

"Stupid?" I sputtered, but he'd already hung up.

I returned to the living room, carrying a damp dishcloth, broom, and dustpan. Vinnie was on the phone. Jules didn't seem angry. Had Malika said something to her? Or had she overheard my bizarre conversation and realized what a mess my life was and decided to go easier on me?

"Sorry," Jules said. "I've been a royal B."

"You have. But I still shouldn't have thrown that mug."

"Who was that?" asked Malika.

"My Number One Fan," I said. "He's at my place."

"Call the cops!"

"That'll attract the media. I can't handle more attention right now. Eventually, he'll get bored and go away."

Mali shook her head. "I don't think you should just ignore it!"

I shrugged. What else could I say to them? My bandmates glanced at each other in confusion. I was too exhausted to lie anymore, so I focused on cleaning up the chunks of Mali's broken mug instead.

"Where can I buy you another one of these?" I asked.

She waved a hand. "Already forgotten."

Her forgiveness made tears spring to my eyes. I dropped the shards in the garbage and returned to the living room. To my surprise, Jules jumped up and hugged me. I remembered why I loved both of these girls so much.

Vinnie hung up his phone and told us to get back to business. We decided to go for the festival in Miami rather than Phoenix—it was closer to the shows on either side—then dealt with the remaining business items, which mostly involved scheduling media interviews and the next few rehearsals.

When we finished, Vinnie pulled me aside to ask if I could meet up for media prep before the Wanda interview tomorrow. I brushed him off, saying I was fine. He wasn't happy about that but didn't push it, just reminded me to be early and to wear something hot. I stuck out my tongue and said my plan was to wear a potato sack.

After he left we spent half an hour working through the changes to "Cry Little Soldiers." Then it was time to pack up and head down to the Cake Shop for our concert.

When our cab got there, I headed for the dressing room—a glorified closet—determined to prepare myself for the hot lights. The stage manager agreed to turn on the AC, position a strong fan on me onstage, and bring me five bottles of cold water, a bowl of ice, a dozen of those cold packs that athletes use when they get injured, and a double order of chicken fingers (hold the fries) from the bar down the street. He was used to "the talent" requesting strange things, so he didn't ask questions, just went off to get the supplies.

While I waited for him to return, I removed as many layers of clothing as possible. Being comfortable was my only concern, so my inner wolf wouldn't decide to reveal herself. When the opening act played, I chilled beneath an overhead vent, drinking my ice water, snacking on chicken, and generally psyching myself up. Jules and Mali took off because the room was too cold, but they didn't complain. At least not to my face.

Soon enough, it was our turn. I stuffed cold packs in my bra before pulling on my T-shirt and tucked a couple under the waist of my miniskirt, knowing my body must look ridiculously lumpy. I carried my bowl of ice and bottles of water out onto the small stage. Despite all the prep, I started sweating the second the lights hit me. I clamped my eyes shut. The roar of the crowd rose as I stumbled blindly to the stool where Janis waited faithfully and set my stash on a table. My eyelids felt glued together. I pried them open and attempted to smile. I was pretty sure it looked ferocious.

We'd played here dozens of times. I knew half of the people whose collective scent was overpowering me with perfume and deodorant and hormones and body odor. Bottle caps popped off, glasses clinked, and voices rose and fell each time one of us did something like, say, pick up an instrument.

Jules made it all look so easy. She flirted with the crowd, teased them, and dared them to respond. Meanwhile, I perched on my stool, staring down at my feet, breathing rhythmically, and praying I could keep myself calm. The cool air shooting at me helped. So did chugging a frosty bottle of water until the lights signaled the beginning of our first song.

I put down the empty bottle and began to pick out my bass line. Beside me, Malika's sticks flipped and bounced on the drums. Jules's hands slid along her keyboard and then her silky voice joined in. My shoulder muscles loosened, and my feet started tapping. I stood up and danced. I never dance!

After the third song, I chugged another bottle of water. It felt like honey sliding down my throat. Playing live was a natural high. I couldn't remember the last time I'd relaxed and enjoyed myself so much. Jules and Malika stumbled more than usual, but I lived and breathed the bass line, setting the pace and increasing the tempo to a fever pitch in the fast numbers. When the lights dimmed, the crowd hushed, and I floated off the stage. Blood rushed through my veins.

Once the door to the hallway shut, I turned to Jules and Malika, grinned—and came thudding back down to Earth. Jules was furious again. Malika looked kind of upset, too. She wouldn't meet my eyes.

"What was that?" asked Jules.

"What's wrong?"

"You sped up every single song," said Malika softly.

"Yeah, but they sounded great—I'm so over the Top-Forty pop garbage Vinnie wants us to play these days."

"Everybody loves our songs. Are you on crack?" said Jules.

"No!"

"You're not a goddamned solo artist! Yet. I'm sorry you're going through rough stuff these days, but you made us look like assholes out there. Why didn't you bother to check if we could keep up?"

"Bass is much easier to play fast than drums," added Malika.

"My hands are *on fire*," said Jules. "I think I've got tendonitis, thanks to you. We sounded like shit. What a mess!"

Malika stared sullenly at the wall. I'd royally screwed things up. Again.

"You must be high," Jules continued, throwing her hands in the air. "There's no other explanation."

"I just didn't realize. I thought we were having fun."

"Fun? You also stomped all over my space on the stage. Dancing or whatever you want to call it. I couldn't do any of my routines because you were everywhere! A total spaz."

"Listen, I'm really sorry!"

Jules's face was tight. Like she was about to cry. "Everyone already knows you're the talented one in this band. The genius who writes the songs but hides in the background. Guess now you want to be in the spotlight, too. I don't even blame you."

"That's not true," I protested. "You guys are amazing. It won't happen again."

"We couldn't keep up," muttered Malika.

Any remnants of adrenaline left my body. It was a lot easier to deflect Jules's anger than Malika's self-doubt. Had I really been that selfish and made my bandmates look bad?

"Oh, great. They're clapping for more," said Malika, opening the stage door a crack.

"Didn't they notice how horrible we sounded?" grumbled Jules.

"You up for trying 'Not Your Princess'?" asked Malika. "It's what they want."

"I guess," I said.

I trudged behind them, back onto the stage. I didn't dare raise my bass until Jules gave me a cue. Once I began playing, it was actually difficult to hold myself to the tempo. To rein in my desire to speed up, I had to play like a robot. The crowd was bopping and singing along. We played a second encore, and then a third. People seemed happy with the show. But I felt sick by the time it was all over, and I was sweating rivers. What was I going to do next time? *If* there was a next time.

CHAPTER 14

IN MY DRESSING-ROOM CLOSET, standing beneath the AC vent, I used the breathing exercise Françoise had taught me to keep from changing. The stress of upsetting Mali and Jules was triggering my wolf's fight-or-flight instinct in a serious way.

As soon as I went out into the bar, wearing my hooded sweatshirt just in case, camera flashes exploded in my face. People mobbed me, asking questions and telling me how awesome I was. I mumbled polite responses, ignored the photographers as much as possible, and scrawled a few signatures as I scanned the room for my bandmates.

Jules and Mali were sitting at a small table in a bright elevated corner that gave the illusion they were still onstage. Harris was with them. *Perfect.*

As I picked my way through the crowd toward them, someone put a hand on my shoulder. I spun around and smacked the hand away. But it was just some girl who looked about twelve holding out a concert flyer, a *New York* magazine interview we'd done, and then, inexplicably, a baby's onesie.

"Sam Lee! Ohmigod!" she gushed. "You didn't leave! Ohmigod, ohmigod. You always leave! Please . . . oh, dear goddess, sign these . . . sign?"

I signed them all, grateful she didn't make a big deal about my

mini panic attack or launch into the story behind the baby clothes. Then I pulled up a chair beside Mali and hunched over the table with my back to the room, hopefully giving off the vibe that everyone else should leave me alone.

Tanis wandered over to take our orders and pointed the severely underage girl toward the door.

"What do you want?" she drawled, cutting slit-like eyes from me to Harris and back again.

"Coke," said Jules.

"Checker Cab Blonde," said Harris. He'd clearly had a head start on everyone during the concert and was very happy to see me—*too* happy. He was leering drunkenly. A repeat performance.

"You want anything?" she asked me and Malika.

"Coffee," said Mali.

"Lemongrass mint tea," I said. "And anything you have that's meat."

"Meat?"

"Yeah. Tuna salad, hold the bread, or chicken salad with no lettuce. Whatever."

"We don't sell meat. We have cupcakes. And pumpkin whoopee pies."

"Forget it."

She grimaced and huffed off, probably planning to lace my tea with arsenic. I slouched even more. "So," I said, "I guess I should tell everyone that I am, in fact, eating meat again. The gossip is right, for once."

"Well, there goes your deal for that PETA public service announcement," said Jules. "It was great free promo."

"I made tofu bacon for you this morning!" said Malika.

"And I really appreciated it. I'd still be vegetarian if, uh, the doctor didn't tell me my body needs more protein and, uh, iron. Doctor's orders, right? What can you do? It will help me feel better."

Mali looked away—a telltale sign that all was not well.

"She ate enough sashimi for three people on our date," slurred Harris.

"You two went on a date?" said Jules. "What about Marie?"

"Broke up," he said. "Through. Finished. Ka-put!"

"So that's why she's hovering near the bar, staring at us," said Jules.

We all turned at once. When Marie saw us looking, she turned to the bar. My favorite waitress handed her a shot of what looked like vodka. Marie slammed it down, then wiped her mouth.

"Maybe all that meat is what's making you sick," suggested Jules.

I could've used a gushing fan right then to distract them. I scanned around, hoping one of the familiar faces would come save me. My eyes skipped back to Marie, who was staring again, then landed on another person nearby who was also staring. *Marlon?* As soon as we made eye contact, he shoved off the bar and wound his way toward us. He was wearing a soft gray T-shirt, purple pants, and black high-tops. He moved through the crowd so lithely, I could see his inner wolf.

The closer Marlon came, the more I panicked. I scooted toward Harris until our knees touched. He reached over and rested a possessive hand on mine. Though I was tempted to push it off, I resisted. It felt safer having people—Marlon—assume we were a couple.

Marlon peered down at my hand with a sour expression, then simply reached out and claimed my shoulder. Damn men! I shrugged his hand away. He grabbed a chair and shoved it between me and

Malika—creating a Sam Sandwich between him and Harris—and flashed them all a wicked grin. Jules melted a little, I could tell. Traitor! Malika's eyes narrowed. Harris scowled.

"Hey, Marlon," said Harris, obviously not thrilled to see him.

"Mind if I join you guys?" Marlon asked, although he was already sitting.

"Yes," I said. "I do, actually."

He ignored me and looked around for the waitress.

"Why are you stalking Sam?" asked Malika.

"I'm not stalking anyone," responded Marlon.

"You broke into her apartment!"

"To *protect* her," he said, leaning over to whisper into my ear. "From my brother. That's why I'm here tonight. I think he might come after you."

"Why?" I whispered back.

"He's obsessed with you. My parents have decided to send him away. Somewhere he'll get help—a rehab facility for . . . people like us. But we have to catch him first. You can relax, though. I'll be here to handle him if he shows up." Marlon glanced warily around the room, then spoke louder for everyone's benefit. "Great show, by the way. I like how you sped up the songs. Got people dancing."

"That was a mistake," said Jules, smiling flirtatiously. I could practically hear her thinking: *I'd like him to stalk* me *for a while. Ooo-weee.* I stifled a snarl.

Marlon seemed to be oblivious. He was more interested in Harris. "I warned you to stay away from Sam."

Harris sniffed. "It's none of your business."

"It *is* my business. It could end very badly for you!"

"That's a risk Sam and I will have to decide on. Alone."

Thankfully, Tanis showed up with our drinks. She took in the two guys flanking me and shook her head, implying that she didn't understand my appeal. I moved away from Harris, not wanting to upset Marie more than necessary.

Jules was openly drooling over Marlon now. I gave a low howl of frustration, knowing the music would drown out the noise. Desperate for her to back off, I pulled up my sleeve and waved the scar in her face. It didn't get the result I was hoping for—the damn thing was so faded it looked months old.

"What's that?" said Jules.

"His brother did this!"

"Cut you?"

"Even worse, bit me. He may be cute, but he can't be trusted. No one in his family can."

"You think I'm cute?" asked Marlon.

"Shut up."

"I don't know why you're telling me that," said Jules.

"You're totally lusting after him. I can smell it on you."

"Eww," she squealed.

"I thought you said a dog bit you," chipped in Harris.

"Yeah, that's what I thought. But it was his brother!"

They all stared at my healed arm in confusion.

"He's a— He bit me while he was wearing a dog suit."

"A *dog* suit?" echoed Jules. "What the hell are you talking about?"

Someone shoved a camera into my face, and the flash exploded three times. After the white ball of light faded, I could see it was a photographer from a gossip site. Rage spiked through me. My lips curled back, and my skin prickled. My cheeks already felt fuzzy. My nails were growing. I had to calm down. I pulled my hood over my forehead and focused inward, ignoring my friends' stares.

The flash went off again, and again. What if the photographer got an angle beneath my hood? Marlon jumped from his seat. Blinded by the light, I only caught a glimpse of the paparazzo running out the door, followed closely by Marlon.

A growl ripped from my throat. My pointy teeth poked into my bottom lip. I licked away blood.

"I'm really worried about you," said Malika, staring at my mouth.

"Me, too," said Harris.

"Count me in," said Jules. "Drugs, and binge eating, and cutting. I had no idea what you were going through."

"Come on! How long have you guys known me? I'm telling you this is all because of the changes my body's going through—"

"What changes?" asked Malika.

Jules stiffened. Harris's jaw dropped. Oh, crap. I couldn't win.

"No! Don't you think I'd tell you if I were pregnant?"

"Yeah," mumbled Malika, though she didn't sound positive.

"I have no clue what you'd do or not do anymore," muttered Jules.

"I'm not pregnant or on drugs or a cutter or any of those other things. I'm just a freakish werewolf! Okay? A werewolf. There, I said it. It's out."

The three of them looked at me with identical expressions of horror. The whole situation was so stupid, all I could do was laugh. The laughter quickly turned hysterical—I was whooping in air and honking it out. Harris joined in with an uncomfortable giggle.

"Nice one, Sam," he said.

"Grrr!" I responded. My ears prickled—the hair was spreading again. I stopped laughing. Tomorrow's headlines would either be "Drug-Addled Rock Star Grows a Beard" or "Sam Lee's Friends on Suicide Watch." I felt betrayed by everyone: Marlon and his family; my friends, who couldn't understand. I lurched to my feet.

"Sit down," said Malika. "Please."

"You're not listening to me."

"We're trying to help."

"You just told us you're a werewolf!" said Jules. "You're obviously demented."

I was so agitated, hair sprouted over my neck and the backs of my thighs. I tugged my hood lower. In a few minutes I wouldn't be able to hide. I snatched Janis, doubled over, and hurtled toward the door, clutching my stomach as if I were going to puke. This couldn't happen here.

As I passed Tanis, I knocked into her tray of drinks by accident. Everything crashed to the floor, but I didn't slow down. I couldn't.

Outside the Cake Shop, the street was clogged with people wanting to get in. I staggered past the crowd and slipped into a narrow alley.

I curled away from a couple of guys taking pills and crouched behind a Dumpster that reeked of rotten bar food. Ugh. A feasting raccoon reared up on its legs and hissed, defending its territory. Could it smell the wolf in me? It seemed like the harder I tried to cage my inner monster, the more it demanded to be set free and the more it tore me up inside. I sank to my knees in the gutter, shaking and panting.

A girl came running up. I thought she was a fan and tried to wedge myself behind the Dumpster. Then I saw the blond ponytail and realized it was Queenie.

"Go away!" I yelled as my legs shortened and bent.

She gasped. "You're changing. Here?"

"I can't stop!" I roared.

She yelled at the guys to get lost or she'd call the cops. They grumbled but shuffled off.

"Whoa, man, what the fuck was that?" I heard one of them ask.

My back transformed. Janis was smashing into my ribs. I yelped and tore the guitar strap over my head with hairy claws. Focusing all my rage and fear on Janis, I swung her against the Cake Shop's brick wall. Her protective shell cracked. Incensed, I smashed her again, then again, and again, until the case fell away entirely and the instrument inside splintered. Then I hurled the mess into the gutter.

"Oh, shit. You're gonna regret that," Queenie said.

"Get out of here! I . . . I'm not responsible for . . ."

"I can't. I know what happened to Sue."

"Huh?" I tried to say, but my voice was mostly a bark. Somehow she understood.

"Two other girls have gone missing from nearby squats, and a third escaped with her life. Barely. She said it was Owen. He turned all of us. He must have hunted Sue and me, followed our scent back to the squat. He already turned her—what does he want? I came here to talk to his brother, but I know you're with them, too."

"I'm not!" I yipped.

"Well, you smell like you're part of our pack. What if he comes after me, Sam? I'm terrified. I'm hungry all the time. I can't control my temper. I don't know what to do. Where to hide." She started to bawl.

I had no way to comfort her. I flicked my tail sympathetically.

"I've been crashing in a squat a few blocks away," she said. "But it's not safe. The cops raided it, looking for the girl gang. We're not a gang! I don't want to become a lab rat. . . . Help me. *Please.*"

My claws slashed through my skirt in an attempt to tear open the pocket. My keys and phone fell to the ground. She scooped them up, along with some cash and a tube of lip gloss. I nodded for her to take what she needed. She grabbed all of it and ran off.

I shuddered through the final bone-jarring transformation, then relaxed my muscles. I jumped on top of the Dumpster and was assailed by the odors inside the bar. I leapt down and padded to the Cake Shop's back door. The door opened, and a scrawny dishwasher poked his head out, carrying the garbage. He didn't see me, but he heard my growl and quietly disappeared, locking the door behind him. Investigating the contents of his bag didn't reveal much worth eating.

Another person entered the alley from the street. A male who smelled like pack.

"Sam?"

I abandoned the garbage and hurtled through the air to land at Marlon's feet. He was holding the paparazzo's camera in one hand, and the other was raised peacefully in front of his chest. He smelled sweaty, like he'd been in a tussle. I moved closer.

"Sam, it's okay." He bent down so he was at eye level. I snarled. I could have torn out his throat. "Your friends can't help, but you can trust me. I really had no idea Owen was going to attack you."

"Which time?" An angry *grrrr* slipped from my lips. His eyes widened. He pulled back. Did he think all he had to do was apologize? My last ounce of control evaporated. I rose up on my hind legs and pounced, slamming into his shoulder and knocking him over.

His head hit the pavement. He went still. Much too still. Before

I knew it, I was on top of him. My claws sank into the flesh above his collarbone, slicing down. No response. If he'd been conscious, he would have transformed. Blood oozed from a gash in his skull. I tasted it.

Oh, god. *What had I done?* I jabbed my snout under his nose. A puff of air tickled my fur and made me sneeze. His breath was faint, but he wasn't dead. Yet. I was torn between curling up beside him and licking his wounds, and feasting on the warm flesh. Before I could regret my decision, I spun around and bounded away, leaving him alone in the alley.

CHAPTER 15

PEOPLE ON THE STREET recoiled when I got close. They must've assumed I was a large dog whose owner was nearby. I dug my paws into the concrete and bared my teeth. That discouraged even the bravest from trying to approach. For the first time in years, I was truly anonymous. I'd wished so hard and so long for this. I could literally do *anything* I wanted and get away with it. I considered my options. Queenie was at my place. I worried about her safety but didn't want to risk being there with her until I'd calmed down enough to change back. Also, Owen might come looking for me. And Marlon—if he recovered.

I cut north, staying in the shadows as much as possible. I ran through Tompkins Square Park and startled some pigeons. They cooed in annoyance when I charged into their midst, jaws snapping wildly. One of those fat birds would make a tasty snack. Four black-clad anarchist poet types stopped arguing about foreign policy for a moment to watch me streak past.

Charging out of the park, I made my way through tree-lined streets to the Bowery. It took me a while to figure out I actually had a destination in mind: a warehouse-like vintage music store called Electric Avenue, which I'd visited recently to buy a special wah-wah pedal. It stocked obscure parts and one-of-a-kind guitars, and was always able to get the exact thing you needed, but had an awful reputation for overcharging their customers.

At this hour, all the businesses on the block were locked tight. Metal gates covered the display windows. I padded to the end of the block and found a garbage lane behind the stores. When I was close enough, I confirmed that Electric Avenue's small back window had only a grate made of thin security bars that looked a decade old. I yipped excitedly.

Starting a couple of feet back, I ran toward the window, sailed through the air, and smashed into the bars. It didn't hurt—this body was built to roll and tumble. I simply bounced and landed on my feet, shuffled away, and did the same thing again. A screw jiggled loose. I smashed into it a third time, and the screw fell out of its socket. I stretched up and gripped the metal web with my teeth. Then I tugged, whipping my muscular neck from side to side. The grate came off and fell to the ground with a clang.

I scampered around a corner to hide, but no one came running. So far, so good. Taking a deep breath, I charged at the windowpane, which broke on impact, shattering into my fur and piercing my paws. I landed in an office-storage room. On the wall was a flashing security alarm box that began to wail. Smashing it with a paw didn't help.

Not much time. I dashed through the door to the front where the best basses were displayed. Barreling up and down the aisles, I spied the oldest, most expensive guitars, hanging from the ceiling. None of them smelled right, until I spotted a classic bass made from some kind of dark wood with a pink pearlescent core and lightning bolts of the same pearly substance embedded in the bridge, behind the strings. It called out to me. The way Janis had when I first found her.

In the distance, police sirens grew louder. Springing upward, I used my snout to nudge the instrument off its hook. It came tumbling down onto my back. Ouch. I hoped I'd broken its fall enough that it wouldn't be damaged but didn't have time to check. I gripped the neck in my mouth and dragged it back toward the broken window. The aisles were narrow and cluttered, slowing me down.

The cops were out front now, rattling and banging on the door. I bought myself time by bumping the office door closed with my tail. It clicked shut. Someone shouted that they could see movement inside. They started hacking at the front door's lock.

Moments later, I heard the cops rush in, shouting for the intruders to give themselves up before anyone got hurt. Footsteps clattered through the store. Officers yelled commands at each other. I managed to shove the bass out the window. Just as the first cop busted into the room, I jumped through after it.

"It's a dog!" the cop called out. "Taking a guitar." He laughed. "Must think it's a stick."

I snatched the instrument and dragged it down the alley. The first cop was climbing out the window, and another one was trying to smash down the fire door in the back. Loping along with a heavy object in my mouth wasn't easy. I dodged a delivery truck that swung into the alley and dashed across the street, where I hugged the walls until I came to a doorway big enough to hide my whole body.

A delicious odor wafted out of the building. I'd chosen to hide outside a 24-hour barbecue restaurant. Damn it. I began to drool, so much that I had to put down Courtney (which is what I was already calling my new instrument) while I shook my head to fling away some of the moisture. Could I get away with grabbing myself a chicken wing? Probably not.

Even though I could afford to buy things like barbecued chicken and old guitars, with my new abilities, I would never *have to* again. I could not work for the rest of my life and still get everything I needed. It was true freedom, and it was intoxicating. Was this how Marlon's parents gathered enough money to buy their massive piece of land? Being a werewolf meant I really could live outside the law. No one believed we existed. If the cops reviewed Electric Avenue's security footage, they'd assume someone had trained their pet *really* well. The Lebruns would probably come after me if I went on a killing spree, but short of that, I doubted they'd care. And I'd be able to defend myself or heal from almost anything.

Once the police sirens died down, I picked up the bass and continued along, avoiding people and stopping whenever my jaw got tired. I had to cross the Bowery. Even in the middle of the night it was traffic chaos, but once I made it onto Delancey, the worst of the city would be behind me. As soon as I stepped into the road, a careening bus bore down on me out of nowhere. I leapt into the free lane but couldn't move very fast with the instrument.

I looked up in time to see a taxi bulleting around a corner.

Then it hit me.

When I opened my eyes, I was lying on the sidewalk. A homeless man with a straggly gray beard wearing tie-dye from head to foot hovered above me like a psychedelic ghost. I covered my face with my arm, expecting a flashbulb to go off somewhere. When nothing happened, I slowly lowered my arm, and realized I was stark naked and had better things to cover than my face. Every movement hurt. When I coughed, something wet spilled from my mouth. Blood?

I remembered—a car had just hit me! Craning my neck, I confirmed that the taxi was no longer around. How the hell did I get onto the sidewalk? Did this man drag me off the street? Had he saved my life? When did I change forms?

Courtney was on the ground nearby—a little scraped but miraculously still there. Huh. Whatever this guy was, he wasn't a thief. All his worldly possessions seemed to be with him, in a shopping cart that stood a few feet away. I was the thief here.

"Did you call an ambulance?" I asked, although I wasn't sure how he'd call anyone.

As he shook his head, he plunged his hands into his cart and tugged out what looked like a sheet. He handed it to me. It turned out to be a floral muumuu, about a million sizes too big for me. Not that I was complaining.

"The driver? Where'd he—"

"Hit-and-run."

I sat up, pulled the muumuu over my head, and got to my feet, grunting in pain. The man caught me just as my left leg gave out, but then his hand slid up under my armpit, getting dangerously close to body parts I didn't want strangers touching. I jerked away and focused on tying a bunch of excess fabric around my hips.

"Thanks for helping me," I said. "Can I . . . repay you somehow?"

"You got somewhere to go, wolf girl?" he asked, not responding to my question.

"Uh, yeah." Wolf Girl? What did he know? "Have you seen others? Others like me, I mean?"

He shrugged and pointed at a newspaper box. The cover story was about a couple of prep school girls who'd gone missing. "Who hasn't? They hide in abandoned buildings and come out at night."

I hopped over to Courtney on the leg that didn't hurt like a bitch. Bending down to pick her up was going to kill me. As soon as the guy figured out what I was doing, he came over to assist. I was grateful, because I wasn't sure the muumuu would keep me covered. Talk about a money shot.

"Hang on, Missy," said the guy, rummaging through his bags until he located a pink "I ♥ the Big Apple" hat. He handed it to me, then planted his hands on his hips expectantly. I inspected the hat. It looked brand-new. I jammed it on my head. It was big enough to fit a baby elephant. Then the man turned, dived into his cart again and found me a cloth belt. He rubbed at some ground-in crud before he came over and looped it around my neck. Not a belt—it was a guitar strap!

"Hey, thanks again," I said, attaching Courtney and pulling her as tight as possible. "Maybe I can return the favor sometime."

"You will." He sounded so certain. "I'll be around." He walked away, pushing his overloaded cart.

"Okay, good!" I called after him.

I realized I had no shoes. I dragged myself behind a building and folded the hat and muumuu into a bundle on my back, in case I needed them later. Then I slid into wolf form. My sore leg hurt less when I could put weight on the other three. I played it extra safe crossing streets from then on.

Back at my place, I faced a new dilemma: I'd given Queenie my keys and phone. Awesome. Of course my problem tenants hadn't left the door propped open tonight. I rang the buzzer to see if Queenie was up there but got no response. Where had she gone? My best option appeared to be climbing inside the same way that Sue and the Lebrun brothers had. Hmm. If they could do it . . .

The passage between my building and the next one led to the backyard and the fire escape. It was so dark back here. Could I really climb up to the fourth floor? Definitely not with a bass on my back. I bit at the strap to release it and stashed Courtney beneath the old loading dock. Then I jumped onto the dock to get a little closer to the bottom of the folded metal staircase.

My first hurdle would be jumping to the stairs about fifteen feet up. I hopped onto a plastic table on the dock that was used for picnics and leapt again, twisting my torso in midair and trying to use the additional force to propel my body upward. My front paws successfully hit the metal platform. I bucked my lower half, but my hind legs didn't quite make it. My butt hung downward until I lost my grip and fell to the ground, landing on my sore leg.

Whimpering, I paced around the neglected backyard, hoping that would ease the pain. So my wolf body couldn't defy gravity. I wasn't actually a superhero. But I *was* superstrong. There should be a way to leverage that. It took a good ten minutes before I was ready to try again. I'd have to remember to stash another set of keys out here for emergencies. Clearly, there were going to be times when I couldn't show up and borrow my mom's.

Instead of starting on the table, I jumped onto it from a different angle, bounced off it and hit the platform with my front legs, then immediately hopped. That got my back legs high enough. Sweet. After that it was easy to clamber up to the fourth floor. The tricky part would be getting from the fire escape to the window ledge.

Stupidly, I looked down. The pavement was *very* far away. Would a fall like this kill a werewolf? Maybe. Would I stay in this form or turn human again if I died? I'd changed back when the taxi hit me, but there was no way to know. If I remained a wolf, how would my mother ever find out what happened to her daughter . . . ?

Pushing aside all my fears, I climbed onto the corner of the railing and stared at my kitchen window. With four feet, it wasn't difficult to keep a firm grip. That was encouraging, because the window ledge was a lot wider than the stair railing.

So I jumped . . . and landed on the ledge . . . and managed to stay up there. It was even *less* fun than I'd imagined. The wind buffeted me against the windowpane. I willed my paws to change into human hands. They did. The rest of my body followed. That part was getting easier. Human fingers could grip the window frame and yank it upward. It was barred shut. Marlon must've put the mop handle back in place for me. After a couple of tries, I was able to rattle it out of position.

The window opened a few inches. I pulled some more and slid my head and shoulders into the opening, then wiggled my stomach and legs through as well. I tumbled onto the kitchen counter beside my stove and rolled, sending dirty dishes clattering. Relief filled me as I hit the floor.

I pulled on a pair of leggings and the first clean shirt my fingers touched. My leg still ached. I found Queenie passed out on the couch, looking hairier than ever, with her sunshine-yellow hair splayed across a cushion. She'd been playing Karaoke Revolution, my favorite game. I turned it off, figuring I should just let her sleep for now.

I couldn't forget about the bass. As soon as one of my tenants went out to toss the garbage, they'd see it, and Courtney was clearly expensive. I didn't want anyone to take her or ask questions.

Grabbing my keys off the kitchen table, I headed downstairs to reclaim my stolen goods. Aside from a brief flirtation with stealing nail polish in my tweens, I'd never taken anything that wasn't mine. And now . . . Marlon. Was I a thief *and* a murderer?

After picking up the bass, I walked around to the front door, playing the chorus of "Not Missing You." The new instrument sounded weird. Its shape was foreign. I missed Janis. My sudden rage toward her mystified me.

My fingers were shaky, but most of the strings had good sound quality. They tightened up when I twisted the tuning keys. I'd probably replace them all, though, because the twang was off on one. I fiddled with the notes some more as I climbed the stairs.

In my apartment, I rubbed down Courtney with a damp cloth, scrubbed the dirt from my feet and hands, and inspected any remaining scrapes and bruises. I was in incredible shape considering I'd been hit by a car, but I was ready to keel over from exhaustion. I turned off my phones' ringers, grabbed my ancient T-ball bat, and climbed into bed.

It was after noon when I sloughed off my comforter and crawled out of bed. Someone was in the kitchen, rummaging noisily through my fridge. My heart began to beat quickly until I remembered it was Queenie. She was wearing my T-shirt silk-screened with the subway map and a pair of my too-short sweatpants, and from behind she looked like a life-size Muppet. Nothing seemed out of place in my apartment. Other than her.

"You're not gonna find anything in there," I said, stretching.

"I've never wanted meat so bad in my life," she said, slamming the fridge door and sliding to the ground. Seeing her face, I took a step back before I could stop myself. She noticed, and buried her hairy face in her hairy hands.

"I'm just not used to . . ."

"Having a monster in your kitchen?"

"Sorry," I said.

"I'm sixteen, and my life is *over*. One minute I'm a cheerleader at Columbia Prep. Now I look like Bigfoot's daughter."

"You're one of the girls in the paper!" I exclaimed. "Everyone's looking for you and Sue."

She groaned miserably. "I keep shaving and waxing, but it just grows right back. And my only friend in the entire world is probably dead. I can't handle this! I can never go home. My parents would rather I was dead than have their friends find out I'm a half wolf!"

"Join the club," I said. "I mean, I'm sure Sue's okay. We'll find her." But I couldn't come up with anything more reassuring. Her parents sounded a lot worse than my mom. "How about I order us a pizza?"

She sniffled. "Triple meat. Party size."

I found my cell and put in the order.

"So you slept all right?" I asked.

"Passed out the moment I hit the couch. It's heaven compared to the squat." She grimaced. "We're not really set up. And there are bedbugs in the old mattress I use—don't worry, I sealed all my dirty clothes in a garbage bag. I'm scared to shut my eyes."

"Understandable." I decided not to mention how many werewolves had found their way inside my place recently, including her friend. I really hoped she hadn't brought any bedbugs with her—every New Yorker's nightmare.

"Did you eat anyone last night?" she asked.

I smiled wryly. "Don't think so."

"Find out anything about Sue?"

"Not yet. You need to tell me everything you know."

"I hardly know anything. Only that Owen Lebrun has been turning girls across the city. There were four of us in the squat that were deformed in some way. We found each other by scent, but we didn't know what was happening. We've made mistakes. It's just the urges are so strong. . . ."

"And now the media's out for blood."

She stroked the fur on her chin nervously. "Sue and I got *so* hungry, we robbed a street vendor, took his meat and some cash. A couple girls tried to mug some businessmen, but that really went south—they scraped one guy up pretty badly by accident. Another girl stole a bunch of meat from a supermarket. We finally had enough to eat. But now Sue's disappeared, and I'm just so scared for her!"

How many girls had Owen bitten? Some were dead, if the mortality rate was as high as the Lebruns thought. Was I the only one who'd fully changed? I felt dizzy just thinking about all those poor girls—how would the survivors be able to live their lives?

Queenie went on. "He pulled the same thing with all of us. He comes on strong, talking about how he's looking for his perfect mate, acts all sexy and charming, gets us alone, and—"

I flashed back to her laughing with Owen in the Central Park bandshell. "You met him for the first time at The Puffs concert?"

She nodded. "He bit me and Sue that night. We were so scared, we ran away."

"Just before he got me," I said. "That's why you wanted me to stay away from him?"

"What did you think? He seemed so interested in you. Guess it was too late."

"I thought you were jealous."

She exhaled angrily. "Not about him!"

"So why did Sue high-kick me?" I asked.

Queenie tossed her hands in the air. "Serious rage issues now.

We haven't been eating well, which doesn't help. It's *hard* to interact with normal people when you look like this."

"Do you know how to find the other girls who've been bitten?"

"I know one of them is still hiding at the squat. Her name's Rosa. She's got a wolf's hind legs. Can't disguise *those* too easily."

"Go find her after we eat, okay? Bring her here. Before anything bad happens, to her or anyone else. Bring any of the girls here. My place is safer than the streets. Maybe we can help each other."

Queenie looked thankful, even though she didn't say it.

I hunted down a towel for her, bigger pants, and a hoodie, then checked my messages. Vinnie wanted to know about summer travel arrangements and reminded me that the interview with Wanda was today: "You'd better be there, no excuses." As if I'd forget! Malika called to say that Marlon showed her something *so* upsetting after I left the Cake Shop. He was okay? Sure enough, the final message was from Marlon himself, who simply stated his name and how to reach him, even though I already had his cell number. I deleted the messages.

I took a quick shower, paid for the pizza when it arrived, and successfully inhaled two slices before Queenie stripped off *all* the ground beef, sausage, and pepperoni with greasy fingers and stuffed them in her mouth. Then she wiped her hands on the pants I'd just given her, turned on my stereo without asking, tuned into the worst Top-40 station, and flopped onto the couch to mope.

This was exactly why I didn't have a roommate. . . .

CHAPTER 16

I NEEDED TO GET FOCUSED before facing off with Wanda Kalamata. I put on skinny jeans and a black-and-pink sequined shirt. I left money and an extra set of keys for Queenie and took off. As I stomped down the stairs, trying to ignore the hunger still gnawing at me, the evil couple came running onto the third-floor landing.

"Hey!" shouted the woman.

Her husband puffed up his chest. "Your dog almost killed our baby!"

"I don't have a dog," I said. "And you don't have a baby." Technically all true.

"It had to be yours!" the woman yelled. "Or your boyfriend's! You're just lucky Zoe only has a broken leg and a concussion. . . ."

If they weren't so awful, I'd have felt even worse than I already did. "Look. I'm really sorry about whatever happened to Zoe, and I'll pay for any vet bills. But you've sent me threatening messages, let paparazzi into the building, and caused major property damage. If you want to move out, be my guest. That might convince me to drop the lawsuit I've already filed."

"Lawsuit?" the man asked, gaping.

"You heard me."

"Our lawyer will—"

"Give mine a call. And trust me, mine's a shark. I can afford to retain the best." I was lying through my canine teeth. While they were figuring out a nasty response, I ducked around them and scurried down the stairs two at a time.

Words of Wonder was sort of on the way to Wanda's TV studio, and I wanted to talk to that guy Daniel again to see if he knew anything about Owen, Sue, and the girls who'd been bitten. I hopped on the subway. The whole ride there, I kept looking over my shoulder, worried that Owen would come charging at me from somewhere.

Once again, the bookstore was deserted. Daniel wasn't behind the counter this time; instead there was an impeccably dressed older Latina woman with salt-and-pepper hair and a sharp gaze that followed me through the aisles. I spotted Daniel in the back, transferring books to a shelving unit and pausing to scratch vinyl in the air to a beat only he could hear, like an old-school DJ. He stopped abruptly when he saw me and yanked off a set of noise-canceling headphones plugged into the phone in his pocket. I burst out laughing.

Before he could say anything, I suddenly got nervous and randomly searched the shelves in front of my face. Even though I'd barely cracked open my first batch of books, I picked out one on werewolf mythologies with a long chapter on the seventh-son-of-a-seventh-son prophecy and then a tome about Roman Catholic persecution of suspected lycans.

Daniel came over and sniffed the air near my head. *Again.*

"Stop doing that!"

"You really are one of *them*, aren't you?"

"The Cream Puffs?"

He blinked. "The what?"

"My band."

"Oh. No. I meant you're a new werewolf. You survived. And it doesn't look like you're extra hairy."

"So you know?"

"Well, you smell like the Lebruns . . . and a human male. You really get around, don't you?"

"No, I really don't. How do you know the Lebruns?"

"They're kind of famous in our circles. But my family and theirs don't get along so well. Different moral philosophies, you might say. Here, let me introduce you to my *abuelita* Mariela. She wrote that *Guide to Shifters* book you bought and knows the history much better than I do."

He led me over to the counter. I put down my books, prompting his grandmother to pick them up to inspect my selection. She shook her head and confiscated the one on the persecution of lycans.

"*Abuela*," said Daniel, "this is the newest member of the Lebrun pack—"

"Sam Lee," I broke in, reaching out to shake her hand.

She clasped mine gingerly, as if it were the last thing in the world she wanted to do. When we let go, I swear she wiped her palm on her skirt.

"Ah, the Lebruns," she said, making a sour face.

"Don't like do-gooders?" I asked.

She snorted. "Good? Ha. Don't trust them. They aren't what they seem."

"Already learned that the hard way."

"They think shifting is a disease," she said. "They believe all shifters are inherently violent, that the human side can't control the monster's desire to kill and the only solution is to find a cure."

A cure sounded like a good idea to me—for girls like Queenie who needed it.

She glanced at the book she'd taken from me. "There's a website with more up-to-date information on the persecution of our kind."

Mariela couldn't be a wolf? I didn't see anything odd about her on the surface. I wanted to ask her what her *kind* was exactly, but it felt rude somehow.

She jotted down the web address on the back of a bookmark and passed it to me. "Our family sees lycanthropy differently. Werewolves are normal, just like humans. No better or worse. The wolf mutation is similar to, say, the ability to run really fast or to solve complex mathematical equations. It can be beneficial, and, with the right training, werewolves can follow the same laws as anyone else. We're trying to create a governing body and come out of the closet, so to speak. Live in harmony with humans."

Hmm, what she said made sense, too. "But what about the fact that so many girls don't survive the change . . . or come out deformed?"

Mariela frowned. "That is unfortunate. Though it could largely be avoided through genetic testing before the infection stage. Most human girls are born with a genetic sequence that makes the transformation go wrong."

"You're saying that being a werewolf is in my genes?" I wondered about my father's family—I knew so little about them.

"*Sí.* You were born with the potential in you, *mi hija*. Just as I was born a *bruja*."

"A what?"

"A witch."

"Does that mean you're a seventh daughter of a seventh daughter?"

She nodded.

"Are you related to Armando Rojas?" I asked, recalling the other book I'd found at the Lebruns.

"He is my son. The Lebruns might hate my family, but they are happy we exist. They're sending their son Owen to Armando's ranch in Argentina."

"If they can catch him, that is," said Daniel.

I'd thought that book was about nature preserves for wild animals, but I guess there was a deeper meaning. "Did you know that Owen's been turning a bunch of girls? And all the others are missing or stuck in between. Except me."

"We suspected something," said Mariela vaguely.

"He attacked me twice," I said. "I'd do anything to see him sent away. And you know that girl gang on the news? It's not a gang. Those are the girls that Owen has bitten."

Daniel and Mariela glanced at each other.

"*Qué barbaridad*," murmured Mariela.

Did they know more? Did they know where Owen was?

"I'm looking for this missing girl named Sue," I continued. "She's got curly brown hair, freckles, and one paw. She was bitten by Owen, and now she's disappeared."

"These are mean streets," said Mariela.

"Watch your back, newbie," added Daniel.

"Are you a werewolf, too?" I asked him.

He laughed. "What do you think?"

Not a very satisfying response. I had so many more questions for them both, but I needed to be at Wanda's studio in ten minutes. And I still didn't know if I could trust them any more than I could the Lebruns. "Okay, can I just buy this book then?"

Mariela put my book into a plastic bag without glancing at the price and handed it to me. "No charge," she said.

Daniel touched my arm. I looked down at his hand, not sure what to expect. "Stay safe out there," he said. "I mean it."

I thanked them and left, feeling more confused. So many things had changed in the past few days. But it felt good to know that someone other than the Lebruns wouldn't run screaming when they found out I was a part-time wolf.

At the studio, I maneuvered my way past security—and two nervous production assistants who told me I was late—to enter a hallway with ceiling-high photos of Wanda dancing, laughing, horrified, and pointing a menacing finger. She was known for being fierce in her interviews. Maybe if I acted pathetic enough she'd be kinder to me? A girl could hope.

In the green room, Wanda's episode promo was beaming over the closed-circuit network: "Dudes and dudettes, don't you dare change the station, because we've got a nail-biter planned for you today! The NYPD chief of police is here to dish on the gang of teenage girls terrorizing New York City." A series of artist's renditions and fuzzy security camera stills of the perpetrators flashed on-screen—two of the girls were definitely Queenie and Sue. The other ones I didn't recognize.

"And then," Wanda continued, "we have superprivate, supertalented songwriter Sam Lee, the girl behind indie phenom The Cream Puffs. Her concerts sell out everywhere she goes, but she's notoriously difficult to catch on camera. And in the last week, she's been acting very strangely." The pic of me stuffing greasy chicken into my face came onto the screen. I cringed. "Is it drugs? Or is the pressure of fame getting to her? Find out soon!"

I cracked open some orange juice and guzzled it all. One of Wanda's makeup artists came in to paint my face. Then a sound engineer mic'd me, and a producer started peppering me with the same questions all interviewers ask, like "Who are you dating these days?" (no comment) and "How old were you when you realized you wanted to be a musician?" (I've written songs since I was five and got discovered by Vinnie when Mali, Jules, and I were onstage at a local open mic.) I stuttered through the conversation, more and more worried that the situation was going to blow up in my face. In a big way. On live television.

Finally, I waved the producer away so that I could listen to the interview Wanda was conducting with the police chief. He reported that there'd been more attacks last night in Queens and said that anyone with information should come forward to help the police. "The most unusual part," explained the chief, "is the victims say the girls were wearing dog costumes. Well, one had hind legs, anyway. And the other had pointy teeth."

"Fake teeth and dog legs?" Wanda smirked. "They sound like circus freaks!"

"Might make them a little easier to find, though," he said seriously.

"What kind of nut job gets dressed up to mug people?" pressed Wanda.

"The fact is, they're not all robbing their victims."

"What *are* they doing?" Wanda asked, eyes gleaming.

"We're not sure. They're extremely violent. We have reports of maulings. Oddly enough, two of the victims were butchers and were attacked on the job."

She clucked her tongue and shook her head. "Tragic. I don't know what this world's coming to. Thanks for your time, Chief Fulford. Are there any last words you'd like to say to our audience?"

"Don't trust strangers, even if they look like harmless teenage girls. We're dealing with dangerous criminals, and we need your help to bring them to justice."

I almost jumped up and ran out of the studio right then, determined to personally keep the weregirls safe—and to stop them from hurting anyone else. They must be scared and desperate, like me. And imagine how my evil tenants would feel about a dozen of us camped out above their heads. . . .

"Sam!" The producer snapped her fingers in my face.

"Sorry. Yeah?"

"You're up. Are you feeling all right? You're sweating a lot."

I mopped my forehead, smearing my sleeve with creamy makeup. "Just make sure there's a fan on me."

She jerked her head at the makeup artist, who applied more powder, then she led me out to the stage. The crowd was dancing and cheering to "Not Missing You," which pounded through the speakers—Wanda liked to get them partying between segments to keep up the energy, and she'd been playing our music today. When I stepped through the stage door, I could smell the adrenaline. My nostrils flared. I shrank from the rush of applause.

"Put your hands together for Sam Lee, from The Cream Puffs, who wrote this song!"

I plastered on a grin and forced myself to walk over to the love seat.

Wanda barely waited for me to sit down. "Sam! I just want to begin by saying I'm a huge fan. I got into your music through my teenage niece. And then I listened to the lyrics. They're brilliant and empowering. You do know you're a hero to many girls?"

"Oh, well, thanks," I said. "I'm just an ordinary girl." I didn't add *wolf* before *girl*, but I was thinking it so hard it almost slipped out.

"Just a girl," Wanda scoffed. "A girl who wrote a song that went platinum, who's been signed for two more albums. You get mobbed everywhere you go."

"Not really."

She raised one eyebrow to let me know she wasn't buying my modesty. "Your manager told me you bike around the city and shy away from the limelight. This is the first solo interview you've agreed to, well, ever."

"Yeah, that's true."

"You prefer that your singer, Jules Darling, take all the credit."

"Well, she—"

"What was it like to see your first album be so successful?"

"It was a surprise," I answered honestly. "A good one, I guess."

She frowned. "Sam, all your fans have been worried about you lately. You're acting differently. There's the sudden meat eating. Shoving a waitress. Taking over onstage. Growling at fans. Are you okay?"

"No, actually. I've been—"

"On drugs?"

The audience gasped. I stared at my hands, knowing I should say some crap about needing iron, but it didn't seem like enough of an excuse anymore.

"Come on, Sam. Talk to me. Your fans love you. This is the perfect opportunity to stop all those tongues from wagging. What's going on? What huge secret are you keeping?"

I cleared my throat. I couldn't hide. I had to face this.

"I'm . . . not . . . an addict," I stuttered. Ugh. That was convincing.

"The photos tell a different story. You've been acting kind of, well, insane."

I gripped my hands together. I had no explanation to give the world that wouldn't confirm her accusation. "First of all, in no way is this any of your business," I said. "Or anyone else's, for that matter."

"Oh, my sweet lord," said Wanda. "You're gay, aren't you?"

Hair sprouted on the backs of my hands. I squeezed them so tight, I grunted in pain. "Uhn."

Both of Wanda's eyebrows rose. She turned to look directly at the nearest camera. "We need to cut for a commercial now, folks, just when the conversation's getting good. Stick around for more with the remarkable Sam Lee in just a moment!"

The sound of an ad for laundry detergent swelled, then dropped, and a comedian came running out to keep the crowd warmed up.

"The ratings are gonna be through the roof!" yelled the producer who'd prepped me, giving Wanda a thumbs-up.

"Cut the onstage mics!" Wanda ordered with a flick of her wrist. "I need to talk to Sam." She leaned over and patted my shoulder. "No hard feelings. I just outed you on television, didn't I?"

I gaped at her, then realized she'd solved my problem for me. If I allowed people to think Wanda had figured me out, they'd leave me alone. For now. The hair on my hands disappeared.

"You know, it's really not okay," I said. "If I was a girl with less confidence or with a mom who isn't amazing like mine, that might have destroyed me. Enjoy your ratings, but you are a horrible person."

Then I tore off my microphone and stomped off the stage. Let her explain my disappearance however she wanted. She'd already done enough. I nabbed my bag from Words of Wonder—hopefully, nobody had peeked inside—and left the building, simultaneously calling Mali and waving down a cab.

She answered with "Sam, we need to talk!"

"I know."

"Get over here. We'll talk in person."

In the taxi, I got a text from my mom: SAW SHOW. HORRIBLE WOMAN. BUT SO PROUD OF U BABY. I LUV U NO MATTER WHAT. HOME TOMORROW. DINNER?!?

Thank god for having the weirdest, best mother ever invented. I had a whole new appreciation of her these days. But I wasn't ready to discuss my sexual identity with her. Or my wolf identity, either. I sent a quick note back: LUCKIEST DAUGHTER EVER. LOVE YOU. RAIN CHECK ON DINNER, K? GOT BAND MEETING.

Malika let me in and led me to her kitchen table. She'd made hot tea, which I loaded with four sugars. I sucked in a gulp, steeling myself for what I had to say. "Look, Mali, I know it's hard to believe that stuff I tried to tell you last night. About being a . . . werewolf. But I need you to try, even though I can hardly believe it myself."

"Oh, don't worry. I totally believe you. Marlon proved it to me."

I spilled my tea. "He *what?*"

"You should have seen him, Sam. It was amazing. He came staggering back into the Cake Shop after you ran off, bleeding from the head and looking like he was about to pass out. He wouldn't let me call for help. He said it was his responsibility to make things a little easier on you right now."

"Easier?"

"Yeah. Jules was on the other side of the room, flirting with some groupies. He made me go outside into an alley so he could show me how he turns hairy." She swiped at the air like a cat. "His claws made my brain explode."

"Oh," I said. My head couldn't process her words. Malika *knew*.

"You can do that, too?" she asked.

I nodded. "Uh, sometimes I can't stop it from happening. It's kind of awful. And I have all these urges. I'm worried I might hurt someone."

"You would never," she said. "I know you."

I exhaled—a big breath I hadn't realized I was holding. "Thanks."

"I mean, it's kind of cool. You're like a female wolverine. Anyone picks on you now, you can go monster on their ass!"

I couldn't help but smile. Marlon had revealed his biggest secret to her. For me. It made his whole family vulnerable. And he'd done it *for me*. . . .

"Marlon thinks you need someone you can trust," Malika went on. "He's worried that you don't have enough support . . . and you might get hurt. Sam, you can talk to me. Anytime. About anything."

"Thanks," I mumbled. My brain was playing a loop: knocking Marlon unconscious in the alley, smashing the guitar store's window, getting hit by the taxi. I swallowed hard. Marlon was right. I did need a friend I could trust.

"Well, just know I'm here for you, Sam. I won't judge. I know what it feels like to live with a shadow hanging over your head. You are who you are, and that's natural and beautiful."

"*You're* amazing, Mali. I'm so lucky to have you as a friend." I realized she was trying to tell me something, and I had a feeling I knew what it was. "You don't have to hide anything from me, either."

She hesitated. "I have a crush on someone."

"You do?"

"It's killing me. . . . Marie, okay? Harris's Marie. Well, his ex-Marie."

I jumped up to give her a hug. "That's great. I mean, wow! Good for you! It's been so long since you dated anyone."

"Yeah." She blushed.

Neither of us had to mention that the last person Malika had dated was a guy. Or that her ultrareligious family was going to flip out over this. I hoped they could be supportive, eventually.

We clung to each other in a desperate little hug. Relief over our confessions made us giddy. It hit me again that Marlon had revealed his secret to her—for my sake. A giggle escaped from deep in my throat. Then it took over, became hysterical, and wouldn't stop. Malika joined in. We ended up dancing around the kitchen like fools.

When the giggle fit died out, we sank back into our chairs and drank our cold tea. She didn't ask me to change in front of her. I didn't think either of us was ready for that yet. But she asked a million questions about the night I was attacked in the park and what happened after. It made all the difference in the world that Mali believed me. Still, something stopped me from telling her about Owen jumping me at the Lebruns' house and the weregirls who might be crashing at my place. I was afraid to drag her into all my problems, because I knew she'd want to help. And I didn't want her to get hurt.

CHAPTER 17

QUEENIE WASN'T AROUND when I got back to my place, but she'd stocked up on meat. After shoving an entire package of sliced turkey into my mouth and jamming on my new bass for twenty minutes, I was convinced the songs were going to sound incredible but that I couldn't live with the bad mojo from my theft. I needed to pay the owner of Electric Avenue, even if he was notorious for ripping people off. I'd psyched myself up to head over there when my intercom buzzed. I pushed the button on the box. "Who is it?"

"Hey, it's Harris."

"Oh," I said, disappointed. I knew who I'd been hoping for.

"Can I come up?

"Now's not really the best time."

"We need to talk," he insisted. "Just for a minute."

I sighed. "Okay." I buzzed him in, tossed a cloth over my table's scarred surface, and boiled water for tea, hoping that would keep us in neutral territory. I didn't need any more caffeine, but I needed *something* to focus on.

Harris knocked and I let him in. He glanced at my band posters for Bikini Kill, My Little Airport, and The Runaways, along with a few of Mom's pet portraits, which together cluttered the walls of my entrance area. He wore a T-shirt with one of Jordan Watanabe's

NOT YOUR ORDINARY WOLF GIRL

designs on it: two male Smurfs holding hands and frolicking in a field of yellow flowers.

"Jordan's selling T-shirts now?" I asked.

He nodded. "Only at comic book conventions. So . . . I saw *The Wanda Show* this afternoon. She was pretty harsh."

"Oh, yeah. And I'm not gay, FYI."

He smiled. Before I could say anything else, the electric kettle popped in the kitchen. He followed me in there noticing my loft bed on the way. His eyes lit up. "Your place is way cool."

"Thanks." I tossed a few pinches of jasmine tea into a handmade Chinese pot my mom had given me and filled it with water. "Want some?"

"Sure."

He'd followed me around the table. His face hovered inches away. I twisted and ducked under his arm, like an awkward dance move, then gestured for him to sit down at the table. I walked around and sat on the far side. He smelled good today. Cinnamony.

I cleared my throat. "How's Marie?" I couldn't help thinking about Malika's confession.

"No clue," he said. "She won't return my calls." A pained expression flashed across his face, then it was gone.

He sat down beside me. Too close. Damn it. To occupy my hands, I poured the tea. Steam rose from the spout, white and cloudy like fog. It made me realize the apartment must be chilly for him. I still had the AC cranked up. Sure enough, he hadn't removed his jacket.

"It must be hard to lose your best friend," I said.

He didn't lift his eyes to meet mine. "Listen, I haven't been single for a really long time, Sam. I'm terrible at it. No clue how to act

181

around girls—around you, especially. The last few days . . . I have to apologize for, uh, hitting on you the way I did. I was drunk and messed up."

I shrugged. "Forget it."

"See, the thing is, I *really* like you." His voice cracked. "And like I said at the video shoot, it was one of the reasons Marie and I had issues. But not the only reason. She stopped loving me, too. We were just going through the motions. The breakup was mutual."

My eyes widened. It hadn't looked mutual when Marie was hating on me across the Cake Shop. I was dying to ask if she fell out of love with him because she was into someone else . . . one particular girl.

"So maybe I'm not ready for a serious relationship yet. You were probably right about that. And you're obviously going through something yourself right now. But I think we work together. I feel it in here." He thumped his chest. "I know Marlon's into you, too. He told me you're his mate. Whatever that means."

I gulped down some scalding tea and ended up coughing it back up. "He's deluded."

Harris's mouth tightened. "Girls are all over him, Sam. I've seen it in our class. Even the professor—seriously. He's got that hair and that tattoo and that Mick Jagger body."

"Are *you* in love with him?" I teased.

"Maybe a little," he said, laughing. He reached out, pulling my chair even closer, and leaned forward so we were face-to-face. His forehead touched mine. His breath was warm and sweet on my cheek.

"How do you feel about me?" he whispered. "I need to know."

"I don't know," I said. "It's complicated." Just a few days ago, it wouldn't have been, but now . . .

He lowered his mouth slowly, about to kiss me but giving me time to bail. It would've been smart to jump back and put space between us, but I liked him when he was sober, and he smelled so safe. His warm, soft lips pressed against mine. When a low, sexy moan escaped from his throat, I melted.

Somehow, we made it up the ladder to my bed. I tore off his shirt. Then mine. He fell back onto my pillow and I straddled him, bent over to tease his lips with mine. I channeled all the pain and anger of the past few days into lust. Maybe I'd figured out the perfect way to satiate the hunger.

His hands slid over my hips. I moved down to lick his neck. Before I realized what was happening, my teeth sank into his skin.

"Hey!" he hollered, jerking his head back.

I pulled myself off him with difficulty, tasting blood on my lips and hungering for more. I'd bitten him! Oh, god. No. Did that mean he was going to become a werewolf, too? I forced his head to one side and peered at the skin. It was smooth and unbroken. Then I realized my bottom lip was throbbing. I'd pushed my teeth into it so hard I broke the skin. It was *my* blood, not his.

A flood of memories washed over me: waking up with Owen attacking me, the fear of unknown stalkers, the exact noise Marlon's head made when it smacked the pavement, the adrenaline rush of smashing Electric Avenue's window, the alarm blaring as I ran off with my stolen bass, the cab whipping into me . . .

My ears prickled. I backed away from Harris, taking deep, calming breaths. His eyes opened in confusion. His brown curls were splayed across my pillow, and his lips were red and swollen. He looked so innocent and so delicious. He pulled the comforter up to his chest. I remembered it was cold in here for a human. Something

I no longer was. I sat down, away from him. He propped himself up on one elbow and reached over to cup my knee.

"What's going on?" he asked.

My apartment door slammed opened, and Queenie came rushing in.

"That'd be my new roommate," I said. "Or whatever she is." I poked my head over the loft to see her taking something out of the fridge. "You all right?" I asked her.

"No!" she yelled.

I turned to Harris. "I'm sorry, you need to leave. I have to talk to her. It's a good idea for us to slow down, anyway."

He sighed and flopped onto his back to peer up at the ceiling.

I nabbed my shirt from where it was wedged between the mattress and the wall, and tugged it over my head. I tossed Harris's to him.

"Can you just tell me if this is about Marlon?" he asked glumly. "You called him a stalker, but you're actually kind of into him, aren't you?"

"No," I said, but I realized I was probably lying. "I don't know."

He fumbled back into his shirt, then climbed down from the bed. Queenie tore into the living room and flopped onto the couch, out of sight. I could hear her sobbing. She must have turned on my tablet and loaded a video, because the sound blared as she cranked up the volume. Harris shoved his feet into his high-tops without bothering to untie them and headed toward the door, straining to catch a glimpse of Queenie.

I followed him. He paused, then stepped forward and gave me a shy kiss. It was so awkward, it was touching. "I'm not giving up on you, Sam," he said quietly.

This was the Harris I'd been crushing on for months. And now I was kicking him out. I swung my door open: a not-so-subtle way of hurrying him along.

He left without a backward glance. I shut the door, then ran into the living room and did a face-plant onto a beanbag chair. With a mouth full of fabric, I howled in frustration. Queenie stared at me, gulping back tears. The fur on her cheeks was wet and matted.

I realized the video she was streaming was today's *Wanda Show*. I grabbed the tablet and shut it off.

Queenie didn't fight me. In fact, she hardly noticed. She curled into a ball. I moved to the couch and lifted her head into my lap.

"What happened?" I asked gently.

"Sue's dead, I just know it." She dissolved into tears again. "I couldn't find Rosa. I can't do anything, because I look like a monster! My hood came off, and I scared an old lady!"

I patted her furry head for a few minutes, then extracted myself and went to get her a cup of tea. "It will help you rest," I said when I got back.

She sat up, took the cup, and sipped. "Sorry I interrupted your makeout session."

"I think that's a good thing."

While I waited for her to calm down, I wondered what it was about werewolf bites that actually caused the change. Maybe the saliva entering the bloodstream? One of my new books must have the answer. I snatched the one on top of the pile, Mariela's *Guide to Shifters*, cracked it open, and quickly became absorbed in a short section on the myth of the seventh son. Daniel's grandmother didn't seem to think it *was* a myth. She listed it along with other ways to become a lycan, including infection by saliva, being cursed by a powerful witch as she burned a large quantity of an herb called wolfsbane, and being born of two wereparents.

There was a chapter about the rapid healing process (it was a bit like having a nuclear-powered immune system) and the limited number of ways we could be severely injured or killed (wounds caused by silver blades or bullets, and being torn into pieces—yikes—so that the healing couldn't kick in). Because of our superhealing abilities, we tended to be much healthier than regular humans and lived longer—the average were's lifespan was 150 years. Another chapter dealt with how rare female shape-shifters were and the dangers associated with transition. I glanced at a section on the impact of the full moon and discovered that the inner wolf was strongest at that time of each month.

Going online to the site she recommended just made me feel more overwhelmed. There was so much to learn. But the rest of the web was filled with dead and outdated links. As soon as I thought I was onto something helpful, it turned out to be some comic-obsessed teen's blog, a fetish site, or a portal for bad werewolf artwork.

Queenie had closed her eyes and drifted off to sleep beside me on the couch. I pulled a throw blanket over her legs and picked up Courtney. I still had to go back and pay the piper. My cell rang. In a rush not to wake up Queenie, I answered without checking the screen. "Yep?"

"Sam," said Marlon.

I almost dropped the phone.

"Got your message," I whispered.

"You weren't going to call me back?"

"Hadn't decided," I admitted.

"It's okay, I understand. My brother is out of control. My parents are world-famous liars. I'm a stalker, et cetera. If only I could get it through my thick skull to leave you alone, everything would be good. Right? Except you're a werewolf."

I couldn't argue with his list. "So you're okay?"

"You left me for dead in an alley."

I choked. "Hang on a sec." I tucked my essentials into a small bag, grabbed Courtney, and carried everything outside the apartment. "I'm . . . sorry. For making you wait. I've got a friend passed out on my couch. And for last night. Very, very sorry."

"Don't worry. My head's fine. I have a thick skull, remember? Still have a headache, but that'll fade."

"You told Malika the truth. Why?"

"To help you. No one in my family knows how it feels to be you, all alone in this. And we didn't realize how desperate Owen had become—how far he would go."

"He's your brother. How could you not see it?"

"I've been trying to figure that out." His voice was heavy. "All I can say is, we gave him the benefit of the doubt for too long. My parents are mortified and furious and worried all at the same time. They had no idea. I mean, we knew he was lonely, but we didn't know he was—"

"He *should* be in jail. He's hurt a lot of girls!"

"Do you have any idea how many?" he asked hesitantly.

"Maybe a dozen? I'm not exactly sure. Some are missing and some are probably dead."

"We really need to find him." Marlon paused. "It's been harder than I thought."

"Yeah, I know. I've been to Words of Wonder. Daniel Rojas and his grandmother told me about the ranch in Argentina. Sounds like one of those swanky celebrity rehabs."

"More like military camp. It's hard labor during the day and intense rehabilitation sessions at night. Armando's convinced he can reprogram every offender. He's notoriously tough—seen it all, worked with the worst cases."

That sounded reassuring, but I didn't want to know about the worst cases.

"So you met his nephew?" Marlon asked. "Daniel's kind of special. He inherited his grandmother's *bruja* powers and the wolf from his father."

"You mean he's a witch and a wolf?"

"Yeah. And very powerful. Knows herbal magic and can cast spells. The Rojas are an extremely influential pack—both here and in South America. They consider themselves the supernatural police, and we put up with them because they do more good than harm. But I've never trusted that guy."

"Ha. That's basically what he said about your whole family."

Marlon growled. "Yeah, well, he's shifty."

"Shape-shifty?" I said.

I could picture his grin.

"He keeps smelling me every time I get within range."

"Don't blame him. You *do* smell amazing. How did you even find their store? There are cloaking wards on it. You have to know it exists to see it."

"Like the train platform in *Harry Potter*?" My head reeled. "I found a receipt in your glove box."

"Ahh. Well, Daniel's family thinks we can dominate our inner wolves and control them. That we should tell the world what we really are and that people will accept it. I just don't think that's possible—and now, after everything Owen has done . . . We'd have another witch hunt on our hands. My parents wouldn't turn to the Rojas ranch if we had any other choice. But we know he's out of control, the way he attacked you in the house . . . and when we saw those girls on the news, we wondered—"

"You were right," I said.

I didn't know who to believe anymore. I needed time and space to sort through everything. Sadly, both of those things seemed to be in short supply these days.

"Sam, I'm so sorry about everything that's happened. Maybe one day you'll be able to appreciate your new life."

Something inside my chest squeezed. Hope? "Do you say that to all the weregirls?"

"Only you. I want you to know that once Owen's on that plane, he's not coming back for a *very* long time. Maybe never."

I could hear the sadness in his voice. This was his brother we were talking about. I had no idea what it was like to have a sibling. I'd always been alone.

"Talk to Malika. Let us help you. I still remember my father taking me hunting for the first time and my mother teaching me how to meditate."

We waited for a few seconds, not saying anything. His breath became a calm, rhythmic beat. My own slowed to match. It was primal. Damn it. How could this guy influence my body rhythms *over the phone?*

"I stole a vintage bass," I confessed.

"Yeah?" He didn't sound very shocked. "Well, you smashed up your old one pretty good."

I stroked Courtney's slightly scratched surface. "It's beautiful, expensive, and I feel like shit about the whole thing. The owner doesn't need the money. He's a greedy bastard. But I can't connect with the instrument. It's bad karma. I'm trying to figure out how to pay for it without getting arrested."

"Don't risk it."

"This sucks."

"Sam, worry about it later. After Owen is on that plane. My parents are tracking him down."

"I'll be careful. I'm not letting Owen scare me into hiding."

He huffed in frustration. "I can't stop you, but be *very* careful. And come by here after, okay?"

He told me his address. I hung up and rode my bike straight to the music store with Courtney strapped to my back. The owner was helping another customer pick out a wah-wah pedal, but when he saw the instrument I was carrying, he nearly shoved the woman out of the way. He came over and snatched Courtney from my hands while I was still struggling to unhook her strap. He held her up to the light. "My baby . . . she was stolen! Sam, how did you get this?"

"Some guy sold it to me for fifty bucks."

He looked shocked. "Only fifty?"

"Yeah. On the Bowery, near Broome. He was high," I added.

"I'll bet. This little lady is very special! Muah, muah." He kissed her. Gross. "She's all scratched! Oh, my poor baby." He started to walk away, stroking Courtney like a fur coat, and turned back. "She was Joan Jett's, you know."

"I didn't know Joan had a bass. I thought she only played a black-and-white Gibson Melody Maker?"

He scowled. "She didn't play it—she *owned* it. I have papers guaranteeing it. How'd you know this was mine?"

I didn't care that he was probably talking out his ass. In my head, I rechristened the bass Joan. I would totally channel "Bad Reputation" and "I Love Rock N' Roll" when I was playing. They don't make rock stars like Joan Jett anymore. The owner cleared his throat, still waiting for an answer.

"Uh, there was a half-peeled-off sticker on the back. And I came to pay for her, fair and square."

Dollar signs boinged in his eyeballs. The slimeball tried to charge me more than the original price on the tag, but I talked him down. Then I picked out a case that fit Joan perfectly. After the deal was over, he demanded I let him take a photo of me holding Joan. "You're a local hero. This is going on my wall of fame."

I gave in, impatient to be out of there. I felt guilty about leaving Queenie in my apartment. I put away the bass, slung the case over my shoulder, and hurried out just as the sun was beginning to set.

CHAPTER 18

AS I CYCLED NORTH ON THE BOWERY, I had the feeling someone was following me. But when I turned, no one was there. Well, except for the regular clusters of downtown hipsters. In Washington Square, outside Marlon's place, I perched on a bench next to a guy feeding pigeons and gave him a call.

"How'd it go?" Marlon asked.

"Easier than writing a three-chord punk rock song."

"Glad to hear it."

"Joan's all mine."

"Joan?"

"Uh, my new bass. I'm across the street from you."

"What, outside? Sam, that's not safe!" There was noise in the background. He was walking around. "There you are. I can see you from my window."

I lifted the fuchsia leopard-print case. "How awesome?"

"Awesome! Now come up here, please."

I hung up and nervously walked over to Marlon's building. The doorman called up and then pointed me toward the elevators. I headed for the staircase instead. It was only four flights. And maybe I was stalling. This decision—going to his place willingly—would change the dynamic between us. Our friendship would be mutual.

Running up the stairs, it felt like I was trying to move faster than my fears. I found Marlon peering out a doorway. I couldn't stop a foolish grin from spreading across my face.

"Welcome, Sam," he said, stepping aside with a flourish.

I walked in, breathing deeply as I passed him. Yep, he smelled amazing, too. The wolf pheromones made me dizzy. I swayed a bit, and our elbows brushed together. A tingle of warmth spread up my arm. My brain didn't trust this guy, but my body sure did.

The hallway was lined with tidy shelves of DVDs and art books, and a good amount of nonfiction: military history and biographies. The hall opened into a small living room decorated with original punk band posters and paintings. Whereas his parents went global with their art, he seemed to like local work. I even recognized one of Harris's original ink pinups of the *Dream Rage* characters and one by Jordan Watanabe of Wonder Woman in the library wearing glasses and reading a comic about herself. A comfortable-looking red art deco couch dominated the wall beneath the window overlooking the square. The place smelled safe and familiar. I could spend hours poking around in here.

"You've sure got a lot of old *X-Men*," I noted, pointing at a shelf.

He smiled. "Went through a serious Wolverine phase in my early teens."

"I can imagine." I glanced at the movie titles: *Stardust, The Princess Bride, Delicatessen, Teen Wolf* . . . "Hmm. Interesting selection."

"Thanks. Want a beer or some juice?"

"Juice, please."

His kitchen was cramped. But nicer than most in the city, because it shared the view of the park. Own or rent, this place must've cost a fortune. The kitchen had a high, rounded ceiling, and he'd made great use of the space by turning a vintage linoleum table into a counter attached to the wall. Utensils and pots hung near the stove, and mugs decorated with kitschy horror movie monsters were displayed in a wall unit. I hadn't expected him to be a collector.

As I took a seat at the counter, he pulled cold cuts and cheese out of the fridge, grabbed a bottle of ginger beer for himself, and poured a glass of strawberry-banana-orange juice for me.

"Harris told me you're studying at NYU," I said. It suddenly felt awkward between us, like we were on a first date and this was the getting-to-know-each-other stage.

"Yeah. At the moment, I'm struggling with an essay for our art history class on imagery of the wilderness and animals during the Renaissance."

"Any particular animal?"

"Hmm, might be some wolves in there."

We both laughed.

"Do you want to be a professor, like your parents?" I asked.

"Still figuring that out. I like the idea of doing research and writing more than teaching."

"Yeah, grading students doesn't sound fun. I barely finished high school because I was on the road so much, but I'd like to go to college one day."

"What would you study?" he asked.

"Music theory."

He took out a dark-rye bread, sliced it paper-thin, and put it in front of me with the sandwich fixings. The table was a tight fit. When he sat down beside me, his foot was touching mine. I moved away, helped myself to a little sandwich, and took a bite. It was weird to be making small talk *after* he'd seen me seminaked—and wolfish—but better than talking about his homicidal brother.

"Tell me more about your family's research," I said. "You're trying to cure werewolves or something?"

He frowned. "How do you know that?"

"Daniel and Mariela told me," I said, munching on my open-faced sandwich, which was delicious.

"It's not curing so much as trying to figure out a way to reverse the transformation."

"I could be normal again?"

He nodded. Then sighed. "Maybe."

"Would it help the girls who are stuck in between?"

"It should. . . . I hope so."

"What if a werewolf doesn't want to take your antidote?"

His eyes narrowed. "You mean like the Rojas pack? There's no way we can force every were to give up their animal side. There will always be Owens in the world—wanting the powers of a wolf but desperate to find a mate."

Did *I* want to be cured? I wouldn't have to live with a secret for the rest of my life, and the fear of losing control. But I'd have to give up the healing abilities, the strength, the heightened senses, and the freedom to run through the city unknown with the wind in my fur.

Marlon sat there watching me, taking sips of his ginger beer. Did he realize what was going through my head? When we made eye contact again, he smiled solemnly.

"To feeling safe," he said, holding his bottle toward me.

I clinked my glass against it and took a sip. Before I could lift my hand to wipe a drop off my lip, he'd leaned over and kissed it away.

So much for safety! I gripped the counter and pushed into him. Heat burned between us.

He sprang back, nostrils flaring. "You were with *him*!"

My fingers flew to my still-tingling mouth. He was already on the other side of the room. My whole body felt cold now.

"Harris showed up at the wrong time," I mumbled. "It was a mistake. . . . I didn't think."

He stared at the wall. "Forget it. You don't need to explain."

"Yes, I do," I insisted. "He's getting over Marie. And I'm . . . well . . . I've been trying to ignore my feelings for you."

"So you jumped into bed with him?"

"If it makes you happier, I almost mauled him."

He snorted. "A little. So . . . you have feelings for me?"

"I don't know. Yes. But it's a lot to take in. Figuring out what's going on with my body. There's a mutant weregirl living on my couch. And your brother almost killed me. *Twice.*"

Marlon gave me a funny look. "Listen, Sam—"

The apartment door flew open. Something tore through the living room.

Owen.

He stood in the kitchen, eyes flicking from Marlon to me. Then he growled and launched himself straight at my face, turning into a wolf in midair. I got my arms up in time to protect my head, but he slammed me backward into the table at a painful angle. I scissored my legs, smashing him in the gut. Owen's jaws snapped at my neck. I brought my elbows down on his head. He fell off me, catching my hip with a claw and shredding my jeans.

Suddenly, he was yanked backward, away from me. His teeth

gnashed in the air, near my stomach. Marlon had transformed and was restraining his brother. He'd wrapped himself around Owen's midsection and sunk his claws like hooks into his brother's ribs. As Marlon squeezed, blood sprayed the kitchen. It didn't help that Owen was flailing to get free. I pushed myself upright and transformed, ready to lunge.

Owen changed into his human shape and gasped for breath, but refused to stop struggling. "Let go of me! You knew I wanted her. You knew she was mine."

"You didn't even know her," grunted Marlon. He'd shifted back too, so fast I didn't see it. "You still don't. Leave her alone!"

My claws dug into the floor. I wanted to tear Owen apart and the effort of holding back made me tremble. I could kill him so easily now that he was captive. Hurt him like he'd hurt those girls . . . He was powerless. As more blood flowed from his wounds, the smell of rusted iron and salt filled my nose. His face began to turn blue. I shifted back to human, shaking, and was relieved to realize that all our clothes had remained intact, if a little stretched in odd places.

"There are so many other girls out there. Why did you have to steal mine?" Owen snarled at his brother.

"How many girls have you attacked?" I yelled at Owen. "Where's Sue?"

"Who cares? The others are all dead or mutant bitches. You're the only one who matters to me!" His face twisted into a grin that looked more wolf than human. "Marlon's won. Again. He's got the only perfect female. He turned you, so he thinks he gets to keep you."

He turned you . . . "What'd you just say?" I yelled.

Marlon nearly lost his grip.

"You still haven't told her?" Owen said.

Was he telling me that Marlon was the wolf who bit me in Central Park?

I stared at Marlon, waiting for him to deny it. He was straining to keep ahold of his brother, but the look on his face was all the proof I needed. He was my *maker*, not Owen. I scrambled away from them both, as far as I could get in the tiny room.

"It's an incredible rush, isn't it, brother?" growled Owen. "Releasing her inner wolf. I hate you, but I respect you for finally having the balls to do it."

"I've defended you for years," said Marlon, shaking his head. "But I'm through. I'm going to release you now, before you bleed to death; but if you're not on that plane tonight, you are no longer my brother. No longer part of my pack. I'll come after you and give back every ounce of pain you caused those girls."

"As if you could," said Owen, but he didn't sound too confident.

"And then," said Marlon, "I'll tear out your throat."

I backed up even farther into the corner and braced for another fight. But when Marlon let go, Owen stumbled out of the kitchen. He glared at me with a viciousness that made my heart pound. I let out a warning hiss. Marlon growled and followed his brother.

As I came into the living room, Owen whirled around and grabbed an ornamental sword that was hanging on the wall. He lunged at Marlon. No, not ornamental—from the way Marlon dodged out of the way, that thing was obviously real.

"Marlon's always been the perfect son, the perfect brother," Owen yelled at me as he swung. "Everything I do is wrong. I'm through pretending to be a good little wolf. I can't win."

"Who keeps a *sword* in their apartment?" I shouted, scrambling up onto the couch.

Neither brother responded. They weren't interested in me at the moment. Owen only cared about slicing chunks off his brother. I whimpered as he jabbed through Marlon's pants, drawing blood from his thigh.

"It's silver!" yelled Marlon, grabbing his leg, then jumping backward as the sword arced inches away from his nose. "For self-defense."

"Silver?" I yelled back. "Are you crazy?"

Marlon danced around as Owen began to jab wildly. I threw a footstool into the back of Owen's legs, hoping to knock him off balance. Instead, he stumbled forward and poked Marlon in the shoulder with the sword tip. Marlon screamed in pain.

"If I kill you, she'll be mine again," said Owen. "We're meant for each other."

"No, we're not!" I shouted.

Owen pulled the sword free, held it up, and stabbed at his brother. Marlon jerked to the left—thank god. If the sword had hit its mark, it could've been a killing blow to the neck. Owen lowered the blade and stabbed again. This time Marlon tried to jump away, but the sword entered his abdomen—right at kidney level. Marlon seized the blade with his bare hands and held on, hollering as his brother twisted the sword.

"Stop!" I howled, pulling on Owen's arm.

Owen kicked me away before continuing to torture his brother, who yelped with every twist. "Unbelievable. You still care about him. He already stabbed me in the back. All I ever wanted was a mate. And now I have nothing."

I picked up a chair, swung it over my head, and smashed it across Owen's back. He staggered and let go of the sword. Marlon yanked his brother's arm behind his back. I heard a *crack*. The arm went limp.

"Get the hell out of here!" Marlon yelled at me. He tried to move between me and Owen, but the sword was still stuck in him, and blood was flowing all over the place. He was getting weaker and weaker.

I ignored Marlon's order and slammed into Owen from the side, pushing him toward the door. As I approached, ready to change shape and fight, Owen bolted out of the apartment.

I turned to Marlon, knowing I couldn't leave him there to die, even if he had made me into a monster. The fight was kind of my fault. Well, not my fault, but it was because of me? I couldn't think straight. I had no clue what to do. My *Guide to Shifters* didn't say how to cure a stab wound caused by a silver sword, just that it could be lethal. Should I remove the sword?

Marlon took the decision out of my hands and yanked the sword out of his abdomen himself. That didn't seem like a good move. He started bleeding even more. He slumped to the ground.

"I'm calling an ambulance," I said, grabbing my phone, thankful none of the neighbors had called the cops yet because of the noise.

"No! They can't help me. Call my parents. . . ."

He recited their cell number. While I waited for them to pick up, Marlon passed out. I shook him gently. He didn't move. And the Lebruns' voice mail came on. Shit. I left a jumbled message.

I dug around in my bag for Daniel's card and called his number. He answered right away.

"Yeah?"

"Help me! Please. I don't know what to do."

"Who is this?"

"The new weregirl!" I wailed. "Sam Lee. Lebrun pack. Owen just stabbed Marlon in the gut—and other places—with a silver sword. He's unconscious. I think he's going to die! I can't reach his parents! Should I call 911?"

"No. Definitely not. You're at his place?"

"Yes! What should I do?"

"Put pressure on the stomach wound. Use a clean towel. I'll be there in five minutes."

I didn't bother to ask if he knew where Marlon lived or how he'd get here so fast. I tossed the phone down and took a towel from the closet. I held the towel against Marlon's stomach, terrified I wasn't doing it right. He was so pale, and he wasn't waking up.

I called Queenie to tell her to be on her guard. Then I sat there, bawling like a baby as I held on to the stupid towel. This guy had saved my life, but he'd also doomed me to be a freak, to live a half-life alienated from the people I loved. Then again, I'd already been a moody, introverted rock star who kept herself separate from the world. Maybe this wasn't all that different. And I did care about him.

Daniel soon showed up, carrying glass jars filled with herbs. He pulled me off Marlon and removed the towel so he could assess the situation. Sucking in a sharp breath, he opened one of his jars and sprinkled dried leaves onto the raw wound.

"What is that?" I asked, hovering over them. "He needs a doctor, not tea leaves."

Daniel didn't look up.

"It's gonna hurt like hell, but it'll heal him." Daniel packed on more herbs from a second jar. He didn't seem to care that he was getting blood all over himself. He rolled Marlon over and inspected his back. Then he moved on to the slices on Marlon's thigh, hands, and the hole in his shoulder. "He's going to be fine."

"He doesn't look fine!"

"I got here in time, Sam. I promise you I'll take care of him—but I need to focus."

I sagged in relief. "Thank you."

He looked me up and down. "You're shaking. Go home and clean up. You're not gonna want to be here in about ten seconds. This apartment will be filled with a whole lot of wolves. We're stopping Owen tonight."

Marlon's eyes fluttered open. He glanced from me to Daniel, who had pulled a wad of sterile gauze from his pocket and was putting it on top of the herbs. "Leave, Sam," he whispered. "Please. Owen might come back. My parents will be here soon."

"I can't leave you—"

"Take my sword," said Marlon, then he trembled and passed out again. Whatever the feud was between the Lebrun and Rojas families, Marlon trusted Daniel to do the right thing here. I prayed those dried herbs were actually helping. I touched Marlon's forehead, smoothing back his hair. Then I wiped his bloody sword on a towel and left.

CHAPTER 19

I CLOMPED DOWN THE STAIRS with Joan slung over my back, carrying the heavy silver sword in hands covered with dried blood. I wasn't even halfway down when the front door opened, and Pierre and Françoise came rushing inside.

"Sam," said Marlon's mother. "Thank you for calling, dear. How is he?"

"Not good, but he's alive—Daniel Rojas is with him. Owen tried to murder Marlon with this sword."

Françoise buried her head in her husband's chest and took a ragged breath. "*Mon pauvre fils*," she whispered.

"We regret everything," said Pierre. "Beyond regret. We're going to make all of this right. Owen won't bite any more girls."

"I'll believe you when he's in a different hemisphere," I told him.

Pierre didn't say anything more, just took his wife's hand and hurried up the stairs.

I didn't tell them that Marlon was the one who had bit me. There was time for that after Marlon recovered. And he should be the one to tell them. The Lebruns needed to face the truth about their family together.

Outside, I left my bike locked up and waved down a cab. The

driver stopped for me despite the fact that I looked like a maniac with a sword and a bass. You have to love New York sometimes.

The driver clearly recognized me, because he kept peeking in the rearview mirror—it always happened at the worst times. When I ignored him, he launched into a monologue about how much his three teenage daughters went crazy over my music, and how he thought I had some talent and should be singing my own songs, not hiding behind Jules. I murmured something about giving that a shot someday. Maybe he was right.

When we pulled up to my building, I paid and signed the back of a fast-food napkin with a mysterious stain on it. Heaving Joan and the sword onto my shoulder like a couple of baseball bats, I hauled myself up to my place. No sign of Queenie. It was hard to protect her when she wouldn't stay put. I guess that was how Marlon felt about me. She'd left all the dishes and garbage from the pizza and arranged a bouquet of white lilies on the table, with an opened card underneath them. I hadn't given her permission to open my mail!

I read the card: "S—These made me think of you. Hoping you'll let me take you out again sometime.—H"

Harris must have come back to drop these off. He was so normal. So human. Part of me really wanted to go back in time and be just like him. I forced myself to walk through the apartment, double-checking all the locks and windows. It felt like a useless process. Maybe Daniel could show me how to make an apartment werewolf-proof?

I leaned the sword on the side of my tub, ran a cold bath, and dumped in a bunch of lavender salts. I scrubbed off all the blood and soaked until the water got warm from my inner wolf furnace. My new cuts and sore leg were almost healed, but if I wasn't careful, my entire body was going to end up crisscrossed with battle scars.

After the bath I tried calling Marlon. He didn't answer. No surprise. I had no cell number for Daniel, just the number for the bookstore. I lugged my weapon over to the couch, pulled out Joan, and started playing. Music was the only thing that could shut out all the bad thoughts. Still, I'd never be able to sleep until I knew Owen was far, far away from here.

Fifteen minutes later my phone beeped. I pounced, but it was only a text from Vinnie, reminding me about the rehearsal tomorrow night and saying *The Wanda Show* was GOLDEN and that we COULDN'T BUY PROMO LIKE THAT.

I wrote back: WILL B THERE, UNLESS I'M DEAD.

Let him interpret that however he wanted.

I also sent a text to Malika and Jules: GUYS, SORRY 4 EVERYTHING THESE PAST FEW DAYS. I LOVE U. PLS HAVE PATIENCE W ME AS I GO THRU SOME CHANGES. XO.

Mali responded immediately: LUV U 2. ASKED THE LADY FOR A DRINK TMRW. SHE SAID YES!

I wrote her back saying good luck, though she didn't need any.

Jules also texted: UR A BITCH SOMETIMES BUT CHANGE = GOOD. SRY ABT WANDA K. WE'RE COMRADES 4VER, ABOVE ALL ELSE. :)

Maybe someday I could tell Jules the truth? Just as I was writing her back, the door flew open. The next second, I was on my feet, brandishing the sword like I knew what to do with it.

"Whoa," drawled Queenie, shoving back her hood to let her furry face breathe. "Stand down, soldier."

I dropped the blade. "Oops, sorry."

"I found my girl Rosa. She was huddled in a drafty corner of the squat. . . ."

Rosa hobbled into the apartment. She was short, about sixteen, and wore a long, flowing skirt that dragged on the ground. There were streaks on her cheeks from crying, and her straight black bob was a matted mess.

"Hey," she mumbled.

"Hello, Rosa," I said, making sure not to stare at her legs. They were oddly bent beneath the skirt. I pictured the lupine equivalent of a satyr. Maybe this was how those old myths got started? If there were half wolves, maybe there were half goats somewhere in the world. "You must be exhausted."

She nodded.

"I wish I had more beds. I need to do something about that."

"Sofa's mine," said Queenie, running over and flopping down. *Nice.*

"Well, I've got an air mattress one of you can sleep on tonight. We'll figure out something more permanent tomorrow. I'm just glad you're both safe." I handed Rosa a towel. "Feel free to wash up. There's food in the fridge."

"Yep," said Queenie. "Stocked up on flesh."

"Thanks," said Rosa quietly.

"So, did you find out anything about Sue?" Queenie asked me.

"Or my sister, Dalia?" said Rosa. "She's like us and went missing, too."

I wondered how the sisters had ended up in this situation. Were their parents trying to find them? Both girls in front of me waited expectantly.

I told them everything that happened at Marlon's place.

"Are we really safe?" Rosa asked, eyes darting around the room.

"I've got this sword. And if he gets on that plane, then yes."

Queenie's lip quivered. "Sue's dead, isn't she?"

"She might not be," I said, knowing I sounded unconvincing.

Glumly, Rosa went into the bathroom.

I was now running a home for wayward weregirls. How was I going to explain that to my mom? Speaking of Mom . . . I sent her an e-mail saying I'd visit tomorrow, then sat down at the kitchen table with Joan and played a few bars but couldn't concentrate. Just when I thought my head was going to explode, the door buzzed. It was pretty late and I doubted that Owen would buzz, so who—?

"It's me," said Marlon through the intercom. "Can I come up?"

I realized it was the second time that I'd felt extremely relieved he was still alive. I stepped out of the apartment to meet him as he exited the elevator.

He wore a loose T-shirt and pants. Dark shadows ringed his eyes. Scratch marks were visible on his arms and neck. An herbal smell wafted over me.

"Wow, I can't believe you're walking around. How are you?"

"Healing."

His eyes flicked to the door.

"I've got two guests now," I said. I was reluctant to let Marlon meet my new roommates. Would they be afraid of him?

"Oh," he said, propping himself against the wall for support. "Thanks for calling Daniel. I needed his help, even if I didn't want it. His family is also helping to hunt for Owen, but they haven't been able to find him."

My heart thumped hard. I could imagine Queenie and Rosa eavesdropping and panicking at this news.

He winced. "Daniel will lord this over me for a long time. He's already demanding my help in return."

"Help with what?"

"Working in the bookstore. Stocking shelves. Research. And other stuff."

"He's making you do community service?"

He scowled. "Kind of."

I almost laughed, but I couldn't forget. "You lied to me."

He shut his eyes for a moment. Then he looked at me.

"You didn't kill me," I said. "I'm all right." Why was I trying to make him feel better?

"But I could have. I can't stop replaying it in my mind."

"Actually, I'm more than all right," I added. As soon as I said that, I knew it was true. And I knew that I didn't want him to go. I stepped closer and pulled his head down to mine. The kiss didn't end until my back was up against the wall and his hands were beneath my shirt. Nothing else mattered.

"I'm so sorry," he said, pulling away slightly. "That night, in the park, I thought I had everything under control. I was there to stop my brother from doing something horrible. I knew that he'd become obsessed with the idea of finding a mate, and he was especially interested in you. Your music, your lone-wolf image drew him to you. But then I saw you, and you smelled so good, and the wolf took over. I still don't understand what happened. What I did, Sam . . . It's terrifying. I couldn't tell you or my parents. I was so ashamed. So I let you blame Owen. And he went along with it for his own reasons. I should have told you the truth from the beginning."

"You're right." I could've been furious with him. But I wasn't.

His mouth tilted upward in a thin smile. I traced his lips with a finger.

"I've never attacked anyone like that," he said. "Not since I was a kid. When Owen jumped on you, I—I thought I might lose you to him. I couldn't let that happen. I'm going to tell my parents."

"I know what it's like to lose control. How scary that is."

I felt like I was losing control right now. It was either kiss him again or . . . His phone rang.

"It's my father." Marlon spoke for a moment.

"They found Owen," he told me after he hung up. "They're on the hunt. Alphabet City. Near Tompkins Square Park."

That was by the squat. Was Owen looking for new girls who lived there because he thought nobody cared what happened to them? Or was he searching for the weregirls he'd already created to cover his tracks?

"Hold on," I told Marlon. I threw open my apartment door and tore around, grabbing my keys and the sword, which I wrapped in a large cloth shopping bag. On my way out, I yelled: "I'll be back soon! Stay here. Owen's been spotted downtown."

I should have realized they'd react the same way I did. Queenie surged over the back of the couch, pulling on her hoodie as she ran toward me, barking, "I'm coming with!" She'd never looked more wolfish. Rosa hobbled out of the bathroom, moving faster than I thought possible on those legs. Her hair was still wet.

They were steps behind me when I left. Marlon saw the keys in my hand, then the mutant girls behind me, and started shaking his head. "No way! This is too dangerous."

"You really think you can stop us?" I asked. "It's three wolves against one, and I'm packing the silver."

He hesitated, rubbing his injured shoulder.

"Who wants your brother behind bars more than us?" snapped Queenie.

"Yeah. Let's go," snarled Rosa. "I'm *not* staying behind."

I grabbed Marlon's arm and tugged him toward the stairwell. He shook his head one last time, then rushed past me down the stairs, with the three of us close on his heels.

We didn't make it a block before an empty cab paused, trolling for customers. Marlon opened the door, hollering at the driver: "There's a huge tip in your future if you can get us to Tompkins Square Park in fifteen minutes."

Queenie, Rosa, and I piled into the backseat next to Marlon. We whipped through the quiet streets. Marlon texted Daniel along the way. When we got out, Marlon sniffed around and quickly found Pierre behind a tree in the park. Marlon's dad froze when he noticed the other girls.

"Owen's work?" he asked.

I nodded. "Queenie and Rosa, meet Pierre Lebrun. Technically, he's your pack leader."

The girls stared at him.

"Soon our pack will be bigger than the Rojas'," Pierre muttered as he crossed the street and hurried down East Ninth, moving away from the square. "We're downwind, but we still need to be careful he doesn't see us approach."

"Daniel's on his way," said Marlon.

Beside me, Queenie pulled the strings on her hood so tight, all

I could see were her eyes and a tuft of fur. On my other side, Rosa was now running on all fours, canine-style. We weren't the stealthiest crew imaginable, but we were hardly the strangest group prowling downtown at this hour.

"You tracked Owen here by scent?" I asked.

"We had some help," explained Pierre. "Françoise bribed a programmer at the cell company to tell us his location whenever he accessed the service. We've been chasing him around the city, always a step behind, but now we've got him. He hasn't moved since I called you."

"Is he waiting for someone?" asked Rosa.

Pierre shrugged and pointed at a figure leaning against the metal fence surrounding the Ninth Street Community Garden. Owen was staring across the road at a run-down building that looked like it was boarded up. I noticed Françoise hiding behind a parked car close to us. She gestured that we should stay out of sight.

"He's been watching that building the entire time," Pierre said.

"The squat," Rosa hissed.

"We can't let him escape. Sooner or later he'll kill someone," said Pierre.

"If he hasn't already," I said.

Pierre nodded curtly. I wondered whether he'd be able to cope with the fact that his own son had ruined so many girls' lives. And that Marlon had also lost control that night, with me.

"Marlon—we'll backtrack and come from Tenth so we can surround him from both sides. The rest of you will approach from here. We have to make sure he can't run away."

The two guys ran around the corner to circle the block. Queenie,

Rosa, and I crept up closer to where Françoise was huddled, and I whispered the plan to her. We waited for Marlon and Pierre to poke their heads out up the street. As I watched Owen, I removed the sword from its bag and held it two-handed.

I felt like I was tracking that deer in the Lebruns' forest. Except that Owen was a lot more dangerous than a deer . . .

Françoise gestured for us to move forward. The men were in position. We were in the middle of the street when Owen caught on. He feinted left, then right. He was hedged in against the tall fence. There really was nowhere to run. I lifted the sword as high as possible and charged ahead.

Owen twisted, hopped onto the fence, and scrambled upward. Marlon grabbed his brother's leg, but Owen kicked him in the head, sending him flying backward onto the pavement. Pierre and Françoise started to climb. I poked at Owen's calves with the sword, hoping to injure him, but he pulled himself over the top, transforming as he went down the other side. Queenie and Rosa were halfway up, but Rosa's feet weren't coordinating with her arms, and Queenie had to help. Marlon stood and launched himself at the fence.

Knowing I couldn't climb with the sword, I wanted to ditch it. But it was the only weapon we had. And it wasn't mine. Damn. I ran to the gate and hacked at the lock. Metal clanged loudly against metal, surprising a drunk couple who were weaving past and almost jolting my arms out of their sockets. I swung a second time, and nearly rattled my teeth right out of my gums. The lock was barely scratched. Time for Plan B.

Pressing my face to the fence, I peered into the darkness, trying to see what was happening. I could hear them racing around and caught flashes of movement between the trees and shrubs. They seemed to be herding Owen through the winding paths to the far side.

I ran in that direction. If he climbed out, he'd come face-to-face with me . . . and the killer sword. Sure enough, the fence rattled and swayed under the weight of a body. Owen was directly in front of me, back in human form. I moved beneath him, planted my feet on the ground, and held the sword with its point facing straight up.

Owen reached the top of the fence and stood, getting ready to jump. Rosa was behind him. She leapt upward, hind legs propelling her, but got stuck in the bars. Owen growled down at me. His family surrounded Rosa. He looked down at them and knew he wasn't going to escape.

"What about the other girls?" I yelled at him. "What did you do to Dalia and Sue?"

"Nothing," he snarled.

"Did you kill them?" demanded Queenie.

He looked startled for a second. "I can't even find the stupid bitches. They've disappeared," he said.

Suddenly, a sleek black wolf with a small pouch attached to its collar raced up the street. Its shape blurred, and it transformed into Daniel. Naked. He opened the pouch and took out a gun. He fired at Owen and hit his shoulder. Daniel shot again, hitting Owen in the stomach.

Françoise screamed.

Owen swayed, then pitched forward onto me, and the blade pierced his shoulder, extremely close to his neck. I hit the ground, pinned beneath him. Owen's body was a dead weight. My skull smashed into the pavement, and all the air left my lungs.

CHAPTER 20

I OPENED MY EYES. I was lying flat on my back on the sidewalk. The rest of my pack hovered above me. Except for Marlon, who sat beside me, holding my hand and staring intently at my face. His brother was propped up against the fence nearby—looking like a drunk college kid. The sword had been removed. Blood stained his shirt, but it looked like the wound had been bandaged. He had an ancient-looking bronze amulet with some kind of symbol etched onto it around his neck.

"Is he alive?" I whispered to Marlon.

"Tranquilizer gun," he replied. "It's okay, Sam."

I sighed with relief. I was glad Owen was still alive—for his family's sake. Why I cared about any of them, after everything they'd done to me, was a mystery. But I did.

Daniel, now wearing baggy black shorts, handed Pierre a little bag. "If you keep him on these herbs, he'll heal faster. The amulet is from my grandmother. He may look and sound like Owen, but the magic's actually controlling his thoughts and actions. Do not remove it. Armando will do that at the ranch."

"Are you sure?" asked Pierre.

"Trust me. This is how my family secures even the most difficult werewolves."

"Is it safe?" asked Françoise, glancing worriedly at her unconscious son.

"Of course," replied Daniel. "And I'll come with you. We have a private plane for the ranch that can leave first thing in the morning."

"Thank you, for everything," said Françoise. "I don't know how to thank you enough."

"Marlon's got that covered."

Marlon groaned.

"We should get going," said Daniel.

"I'll meet you guys at the airport," said Marlon. "I'm going to take Sam and the girls home first."

Before I knew it, I was in another cab with Marlon, Rosa, and Queenie. The girls slumped against each other, eyes closed. It finally sank in that we'd done it. We'd captured the big bad wolf. And I had stood up to him, even when I was the most scared. I felt prouder of this than any success I'd had with my band.

A burst of energy swept over me. I needed to flex my muscles.

"What are the chances we could go for a run?" I asked Marlon. "Just for a few minutes. We can drop off Queenie and Rosa, then head to Prospect Park before you go to the airport. It's still a few hours till dawn. No one should notice two dogs running around without their owners."

"Are you asking me to come out and play?"

I nodded.

"Would you settle for a limp?" he asked.

"We'll go slow, I promise."

He grinned. "Okay."

We stopped in front of my building and walked the weregirls to the front door. Queenie and Rosa were clearly still depressed that we were no closer to finding Sue and Dalia.

"We're not giving up on them," I said, impulsively gathering both girls in a reassuring hug. I'd come a long way from the skittish wolf who didn't want Françoise to touch her. . . .

"They're lost," said Queenie. "That psycho wouldn't say what he's done to them."

"No," said Marlon. "I think Owen was being honest when he said he hadn't been able to track them down. I'm going to talk to Armando Rojas about this while we're at the ranch."

"And we'll keep searching here in New York," I said. "I promise. We were a pretty spectacular team out there tonight."

The two girls headed inside. I was tempted to run upstairs and thump the door of my evil tenants, but I resisted.

Marlon and I drove to the park. I got out of the cab and stretched while he paid the driver. I couldn't stop myself from watching the way muscles rippled under his shirt as he moved. It went against my common sense, but maybe there was something to this being mated thing after all. He'd made me a monster, and I could never change that. Maybe I didn't want to anymore. Forgive, but not forget.

I pulled him by the hand into a grove of evergreen trees where no one could see us. Knowing he was watching me, I shrugged off my pants as seductively as possible. When I reached up to lift my shirt, Marlon's hands stopped mine. He wanted to help, but he was waiting for a sign that it was okay. His fingers hesitated, inches from the skin on my stomach.

I nodded, and as soon as he'd slid the cotton fabric over my head, I pushed up against his chest. He felt and smelled amazing. When he pressed his warm lips against my neck and started moving up toward my chin, my whole body lit on fire. I almost jumped him right there in the park. He pulled away ever so slightly to help me out of my bra and underwear, and cool air filled the gap between us, clearing my head.

Self-conscious, I quickly transformed, dropped to the ground, and shot across the grass like an arrow, leaving all my worry and stress behind. Marlon followed more slowly, favoring his sore leg.

I darted back to nudge him along and touch his nose with mine— the wolf equivalent of kissing. Then I leapt away again, lapping up the cool, damp wind. There really was nothing quite like the sensation of air rushing through your fur. We looped around the park. Whenever I got too far ahead of Marlon, I slowed down so he could catch up.

All of a sudden he pounced on top of me from behind. I guess he was feeling better. I bucked to get him off and barked as we tumbled in the short grass, rolling head over heels and snapping our teeth at each other. After a moment, he untangled himself from me, chest heaving.

A raccoon lumbered past, forcing me to chase it up a tree. Then I headed over to a stream. As I drank, Marlon came over and pushed his head in next to mine. Our snouts bumped. I stuck out my tongue and licked his face, earning myself a mouthful of fur. We wandered into the stream and splashed around, then shook our coats, sending the water flying.

Everything felt effortless. Smooth and powerful and feral. I was gaining control over my new life and truly free for the first time in years.

I was now girl *and* wolf. And so alive.

ACKNOWLEDGMENTS

Many people helped make this book a reality, especially my mate, Jesse Hirsh. My agent, Alison McDonald at The Rights Factory, and fabulous editors Robin Benjamin and Lynne Missen believed in Sam and worked hard behind the scenes. Julia Pohl-Miranda, Willow Dawson, Lily Tung, Ed Kwong, and Jim Munroe read drafts and gave feedback. Assorted parents, in-laws, siblings, and the little monkey all brought me joy, gave advice, and, let's face it, lent certain aspects of their lives to my fiction. Vikki Law and Siu Loong Englander Law kindly showed me New York's wolf-friendly hideouts. Nalo Hopkinson, Dianah Smith, and Irfan Ali wrote beside me at the local library, in cafés, and at my kitchen table when I was avoiding plot twists gone wild . . . and periodically propped up my confidence. And, lastly, members of Toronto Street Writers, the University of British Columbia's optional residency Creative Writing MFA program, and Sagatay Men's Writing Group provided inspirational and creative powers.

SKYSCAPE

DATE			